TangleEasy

Lovable Pets

Design templates for Zentangle®, coloring, and more

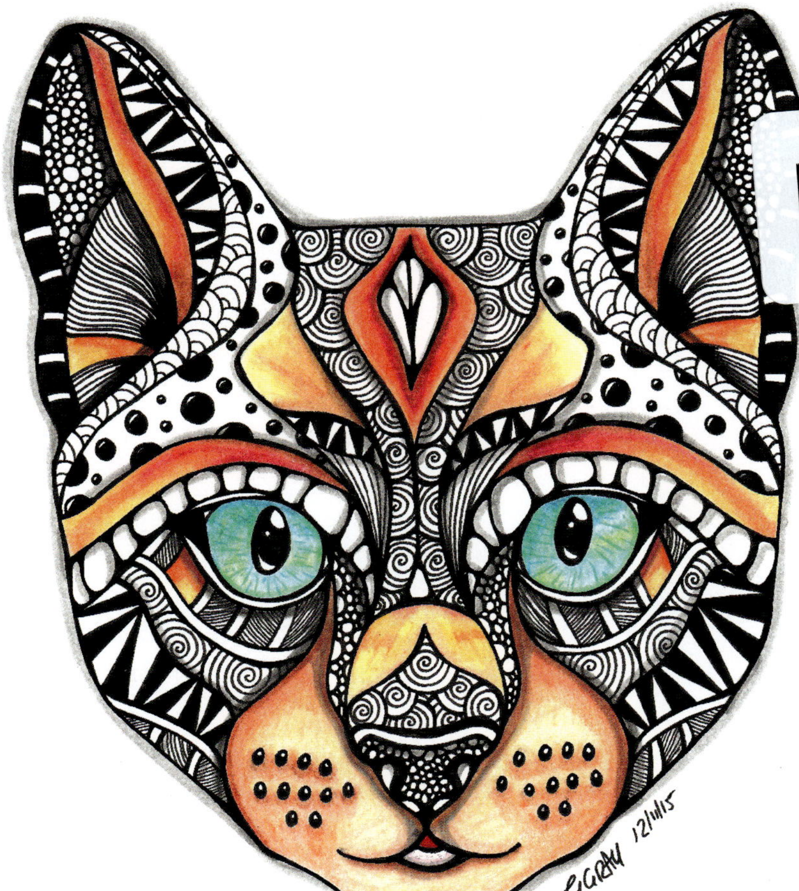

By Abbey Gray (DO#1098)

BEN KWOK

DESIGN ORIGINALS
an Imprint of Fox Chapel Publishing
www.d-originals.com

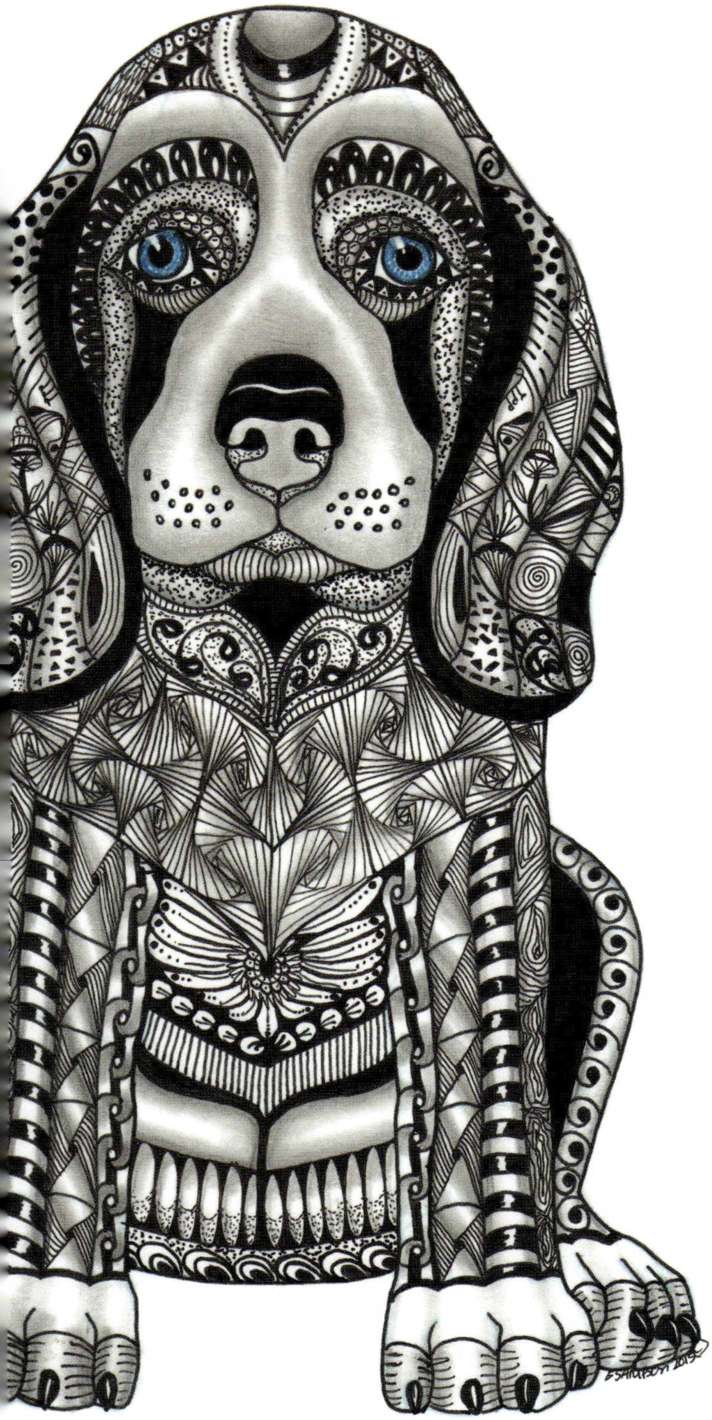

By Elaine Sampson (DO#1102)

About the Templates

Welcome to *TangleEasy Lovable Pets*, a book filled with templates that you can use to create stunning colored and patterned art. Each template has been numbered (DO#1102, for example) for ease of reference. My name is Ben Kwok, and I'm so excited to share these designs with you.

Art has always been a big part of my life. I've been drawing since I was four years old, keeping myself busy for endless hours when I was young by drawing on scrap pieces of paper. I am a very visual person, and while I was not good at some things, I always excelled at art. It seems to be an ingrained part of my personality. You could say I was born to be an artist, so art has always made sense to me, even at a young age.

I received a Bachelor of Fine Arts in Illustration from California State University, Long Beach and have worked as a graphic artist in the apparel industry for more than ten years. I've had the opportunity to work with several major brands, including Disney, Converse, and Lucky Brand. I find I most enjoy art that takes a very high skill level to accomplish. Some people like art to tell a story, but I personally like perfectly executed work. A good example is work by David A. Smith and Aaron Horkey. To me, these artists are the best in the world, and I am constantly inspired by them. I always strive for the same level of quality and perfection. I also like Art Nouveau, Biomechanics, Tattoo Flash, and Gig Posters.

In addition to my passion for art, I have a great love for animals and animal conservation. I regularly donate to the World Wildlife Fund and the Wildlife Conservation Network. Recently I've focused on the Save the Elephants project through WCN, an incredibly important effort in elephant conservation.

I started creating templates like the ones included in this book when I encountered Zentangle art. I noticed the Zentangle community was growing rapidly and producing lots of amazing work. While a lot of Zentangle art is abstract, there are also many who like to make Zentangle art in the shape of a particular object or animal. Many times these tanglers like to have an outline or other starting point to work from so they can focus on adding their intricate designs and not worry about having to sketch a realistic fish or other shape. I saw this missing piece in the puzzle, so I decided to start creating templates for Zentangle enthusiasts and doodlers alike to create intricately patterned artwork that had a distinct shape when they were finished. It seemed like a perfect fit.

ISBN 978-1-4972-0105-7

Cover art by Darla Tjelmeland (Pug, DO#1122; Horse, DO#1103), Christa Koopmans-Hut (Fish, DO#1095), Elaine Sampson (Cat, DO#1098), Dawn Collins (Chinchilla, DO#1099)

Printed in the United States of America
First printing

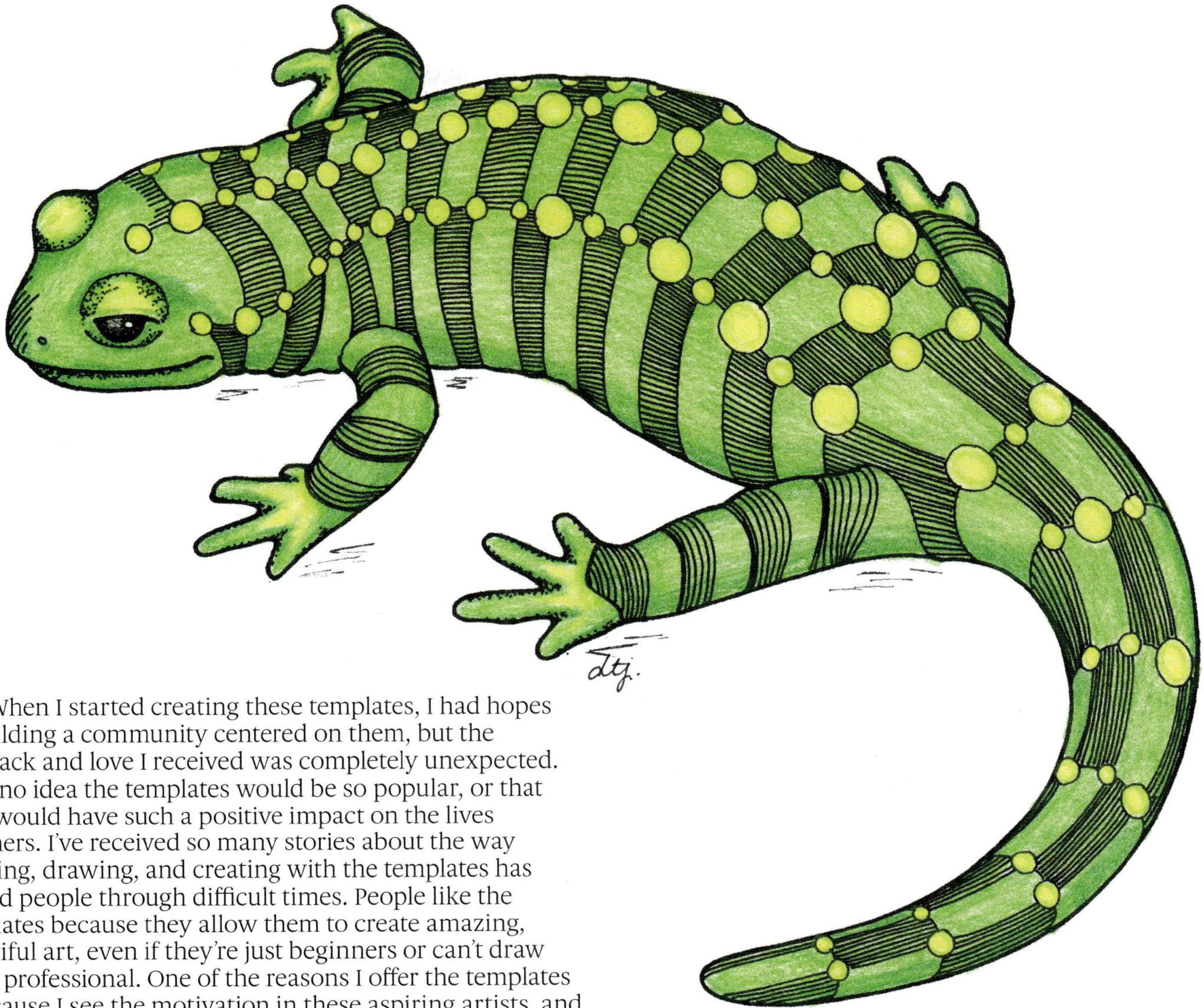

By Darla Tjelmeland (DO#1111)

When I started creating these templates, I had hopes of building a community centered on them, but the feedback and love I received was completely unexpected. I had no idea the templates would be so popular, or that they would have such a positive impact on the lives of others. I've received so many stories about the way working, drawing, and creating with the templates has helped people through difficult times. People like the templates because they allow them to create amazing, beautiful art, even if they're just beginners or can't draw like a professional. One of the reasons I offer the templates is because I see the motivation in these aspiring artists, and I wanted to give them an easier way to create art they could be proud of. I also love creating these templates because I want to give back to the art community and help out my fellow artists. The road to a successful art career can be very tough. Whether you are a professional or an amateur doesn't matter to me. I feel like it's my duty to give back.

There are so many wonderful things that have come out of the creation of these templates, but my favorite by far is the feedback I receive from those who use them. To me, being appreciated for my efforts is priceless. I feel like I'm making a difference in people's lives, and that's a great feeling.

If you've picked up this book, you have the itch to create something amazing, and this is a great place to start. Some advice I always try to offer is to treat the template guidelines as just that: guides. Fight the temptation to follow the lines exactly. Although you can, you certainly don't have to. I think many people, especially if they are new to patterning, follow along the lines because they are afraid of what might happen if they deviate from the template. Don't be afraid to break away and explore what you can do beyond the lines. I think that's where the true magic and creativity happens. Use your imagination and see where you can go.

Through these templates, I want to continue nurturing the artist spirit that we all share. There are lots of hopes that I have for the future—in the spirit of continuing to give back, I'm considering ways to use the templates to support animal conservation. This seems like a fitting role for these designs. And of course, I'm very excited about what you'll do with the templates in this book.

Please visit *www.TangleEasy.com*, where you can see my latest work, access free template downloads, and explore a gallery of finished art created using my designs. For a glimpse at my own work as an artist, visit *www.BIOWORKZ.com*.

Go create!
—Ben

Adding Color

There are so many ways you can color the templates in this book. Use your favorite medium—colored pencils, markers, pens, gel pens, watercolors—or combine different mediums to create unique effects. Remember, there is no right or wrong way to add color. If you're feeling a little unsure, take a look at the color wheel. Some very light research into color theory can give you loads of ideas for creating color palettes. Also, be sure to check out the color examples on the pages that follow for inspiration.

When purchasing coloring supplies, try to get the highest quality you can afford. You'll be much happier with the results. Test your purchases in a scrapbook to see how you like the color and quality. Make notes so you know what you liked and what you didn't for your next shopping trip. Have fun experimenting!

Color Theory

Color gives sensational beauty to the world around you. Color allows you to tell the difference between various objects and landscapes. There are even scientific studies that show how different colors can affect your mood. Color is everything! Let's explore the ins and outs of color itself and how to use it to make your artwork the best that it can be. From the primary colors we all grew up with to color schemes you may not be so familiar with, these pages will show you how to take your coloring to the next level.

Here you see the age-old color wheel. Thanks to art classes from elementary school, it is easy to point out each of the familiar, essential colors of the wheel like red, yellow, green, blue, and purple. However, to best understand the color wheel in full, you should learn the various categories of color that it illustrates.

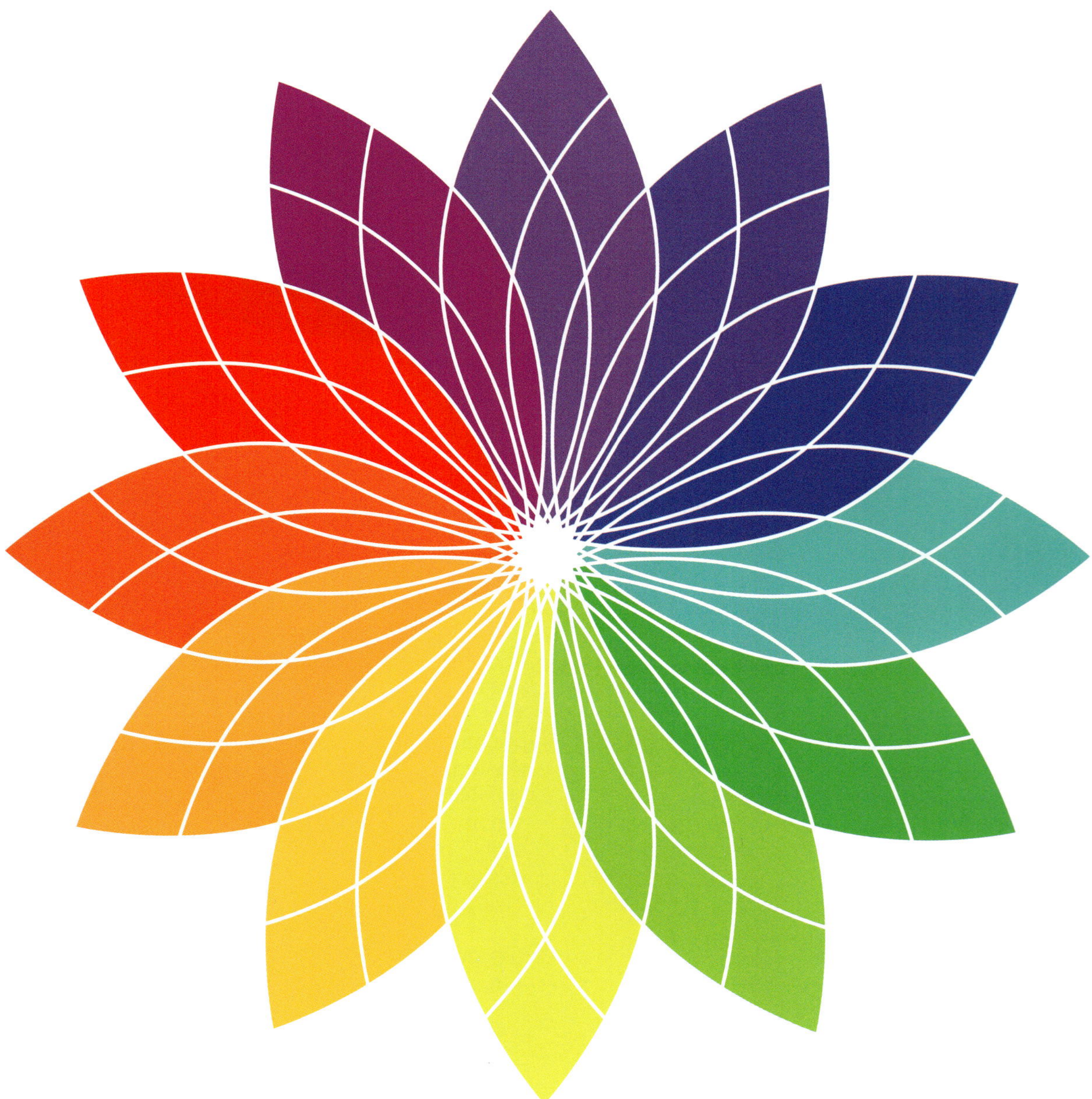

Categories of Color

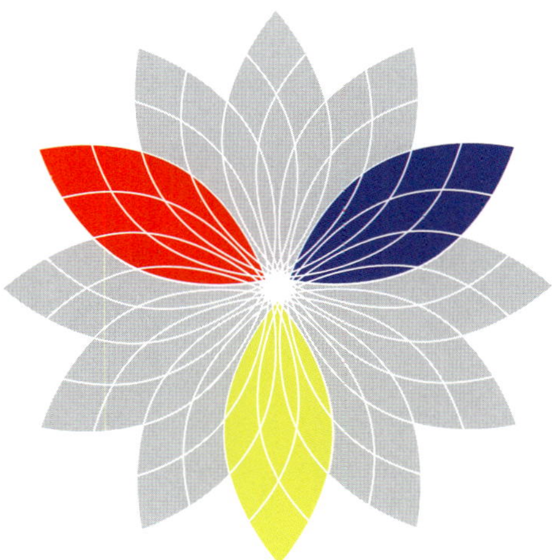

Primary Colors: red, yellow, and blue. Primary colors are the three widely recognized colors on the wheel that cannot be created by mixing other colors together.

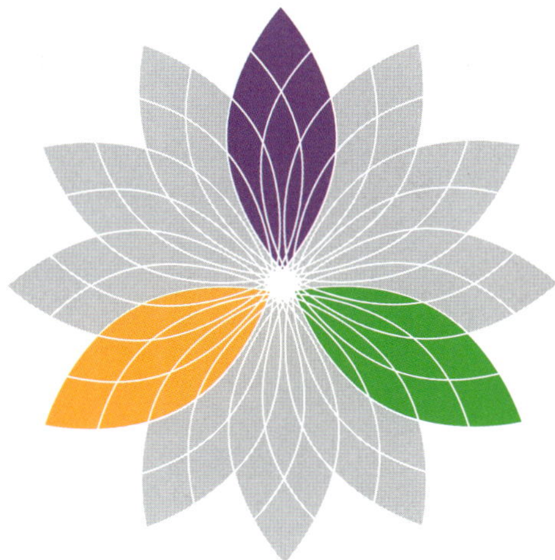

Secondary Colors: purple, orange, and green. Secondary colors are the colors you can create from mixing two primary hues together. Mixing the primary colors red and blue creates purple; mixing red and yellow creates orange; mixing blue and yellow creates green.

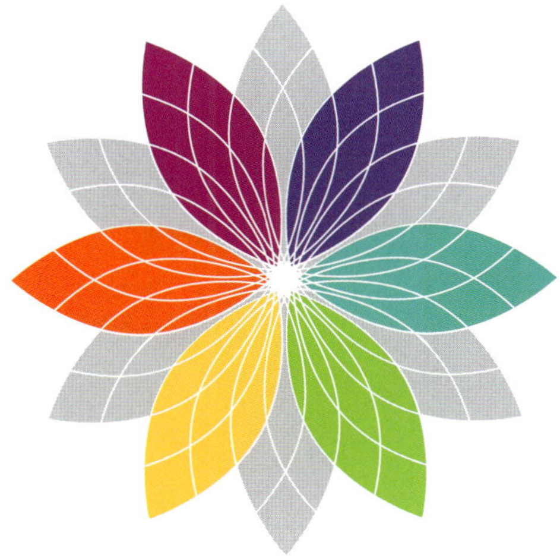

Tertiary Colors. Tertiary colors are the colors made by combining a primary (p) with a secondary (s) color. Mixing red (p) and purple (s) creates the tertiary color red-violet/magenta; mixing blue (p) and green (s) creates blue-green/teal; mixing yellow (p) and green (s) creates yellow-green/chartreuse, etc.

Color Schemes

It's time to delve even deeper into the universe of coloring to explore the different color schemes you can make from primary, secondary, and tertiary colors. Here are a few combinations to try:

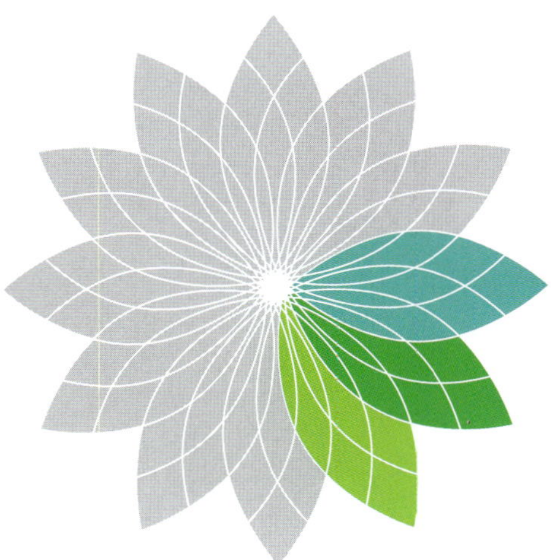

Analogous: An analogous color scheme uses colors that are right next to each other on the wheel to create a completely harmonious range of color. Analogous color schemes commonly include a primary color paired with two of its tertiary neighbors. An example of an analogous color scheme is blue-green, green, and yellow-green.

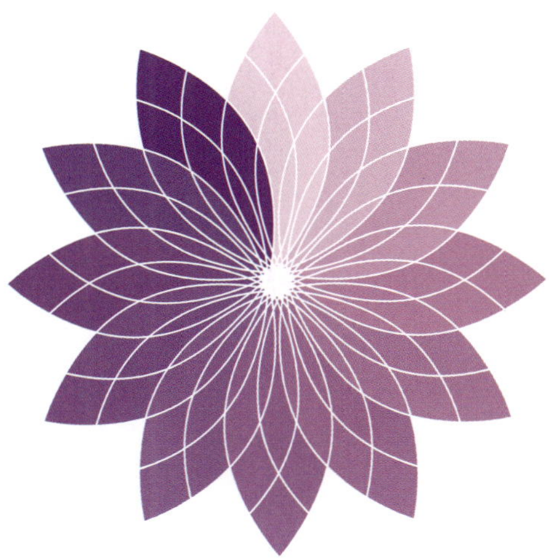

Monochromatic: A monochromatic color scheme revolves around different shades and tints of one single color. Try using light, medium, and dark greens to create an earthy color scheme or all different yellows and golds to create a picture full of sunshine.

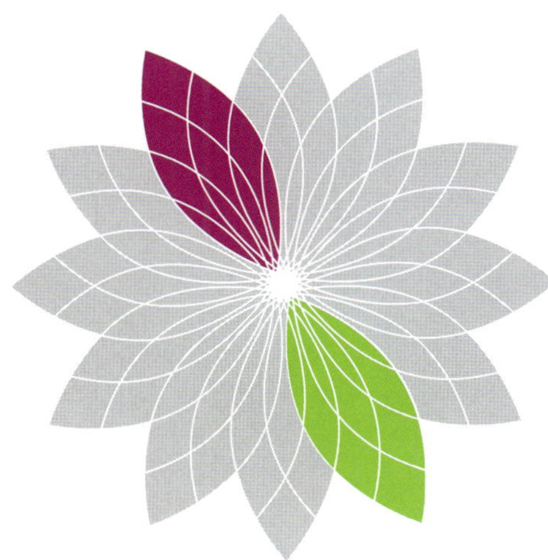

Complementary: Complementary colors are two hues that are directly across from one another on the color wheel; when placed together, these colors create a striking contrast that will make any project pop. Examples of complementary color schemes are red and green, yellow and purple, and blue and orange.

With this guide to the basics of color theory, your art projects will become masterpieces in no time! Don't forget to come back to these pages often to look at your color wheel while you're coloring. Consider printing one out to have on hand at all times! Explore different color schemes—if you like it, try it.

Warm colors. The colors red, orange, and yellow are called warm colors and go well together. Using warm colors will make your piece feel bold and exciting.

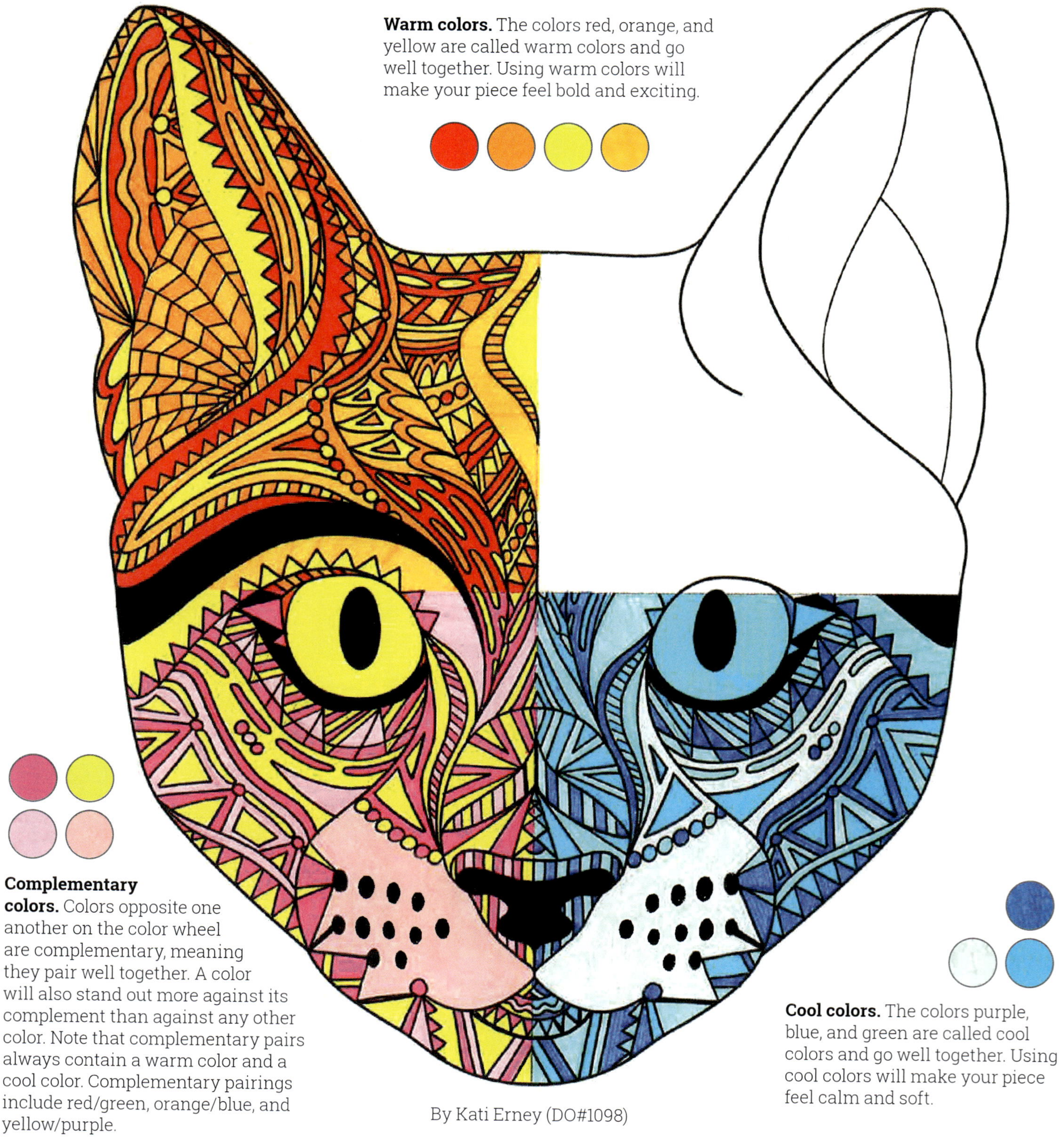

Complementary colors. Colors opposite one another on the color wheel are complementary, meaning they pair well together. A color will also stand out more against its complement than against any other color. Note that complementary pairs always contain a warm color and a cool color. Complementary pairings include red/green, orange/blue, and yellow/purple.

By Kati Erney (DO#1098)

Cool colors. The colors purple, blue, and green are called cool colors and go well together. Using cool colors will make your piece feel calm and soft.

Markers. Markers are a great way to cover lots of ground and fill in large areas. Dual-tip markers come with a large brush end for big spaces and a felt-tip end for small areas. Some markers can be layered for unique blending and shading effects. Experiment with water-based and alcohol-based options and a variety of brands to see which suits you best!

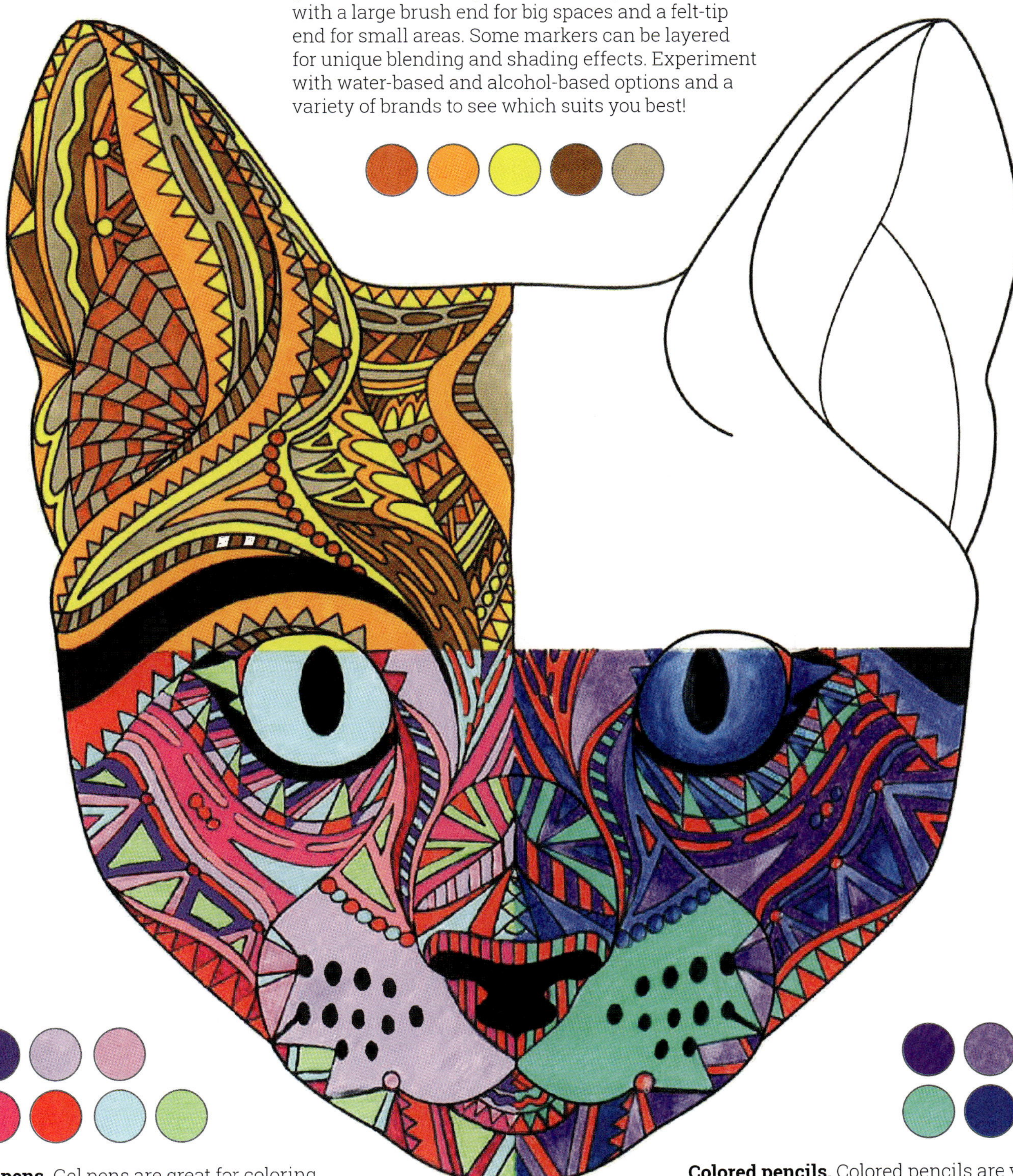

Gel pens. Gel pens are great for coloring in small areas, adding patterning, or adding finishing details to a piece already colored with a different medium. There are lots of varieties available, including neon, metallic, sparkle, and pastel.

By Kati Erney (DO#1098)

Colored pencils. Colored pencils are very easy to layer over one another, creating unique colors and shading. They can be used to fill in large areas or sharpened to a fine point for detail work. Experiment with watercolor pencils to give your piece a painted effect.

Adding Patterns

These templates were made to be embellished with patterning, and there are so many different ways to do it. The Zentangle method offers wonderful step-by-step designs, called tangles, to make patterning accessible for anyone. Try using some of the tangles on the following pages to fill a template. If you'd like to learn more about the Zentangle method, check out *Zentangle Basics, Expanded Workbook Edition*, or *Joy of Zentangle* to get started.

Simple patterning. You don't have to add a different pattern to every section in a template to create a beautiful finished piece. All of the sections in this bird were filled with a triangle pattern. By drawing the pattern at different sizes throughout the template, the artist created shading. Areas where the pattern lines are drawn far apart appear lighter, like some of the sections on the bird's wing. Areas where the pattern lines are drawn close together look dark, like the bird's head. Try picking just one pattern that you like and add it to all of the sections of a template.

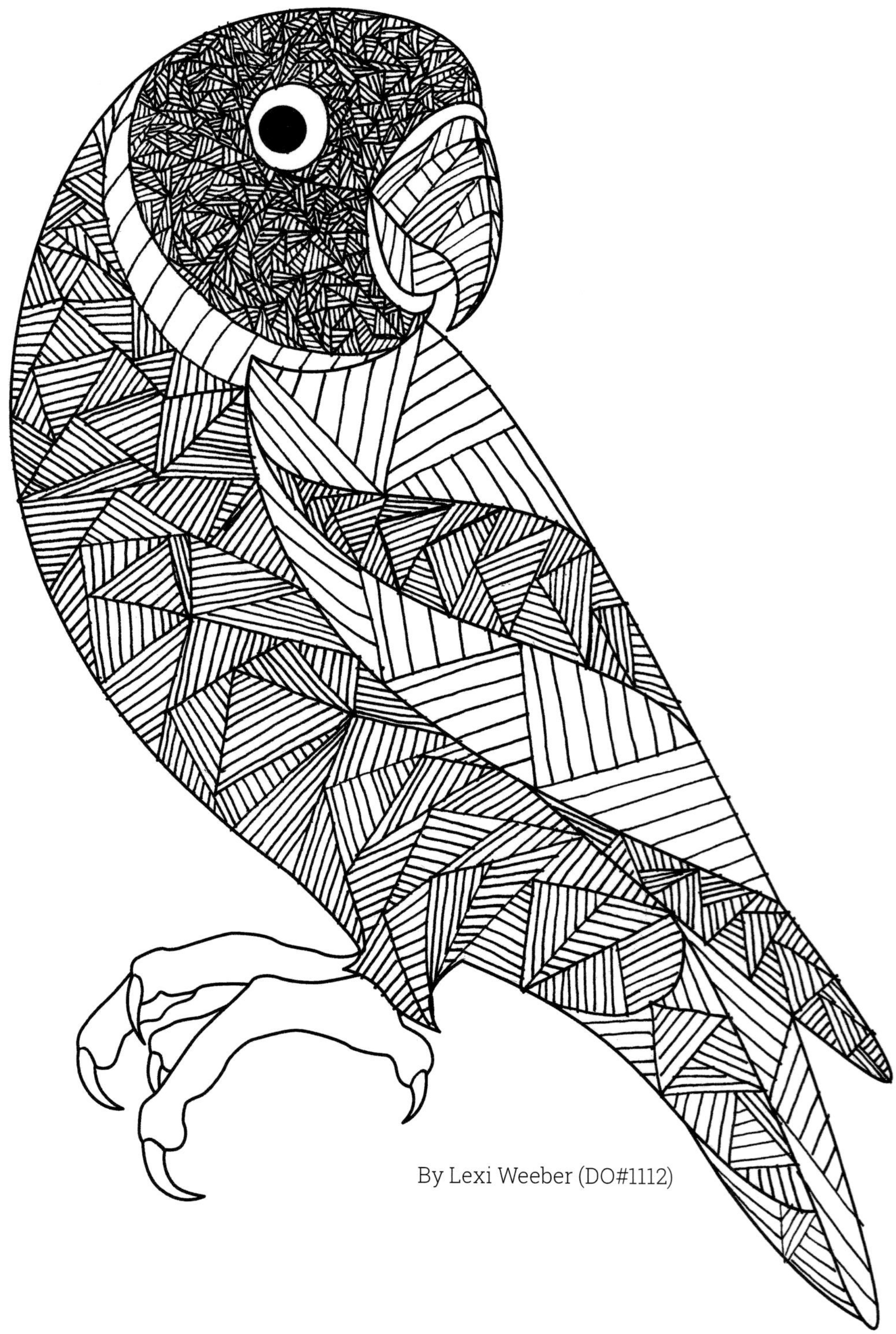

By Lexi Weeber (DO#1112)

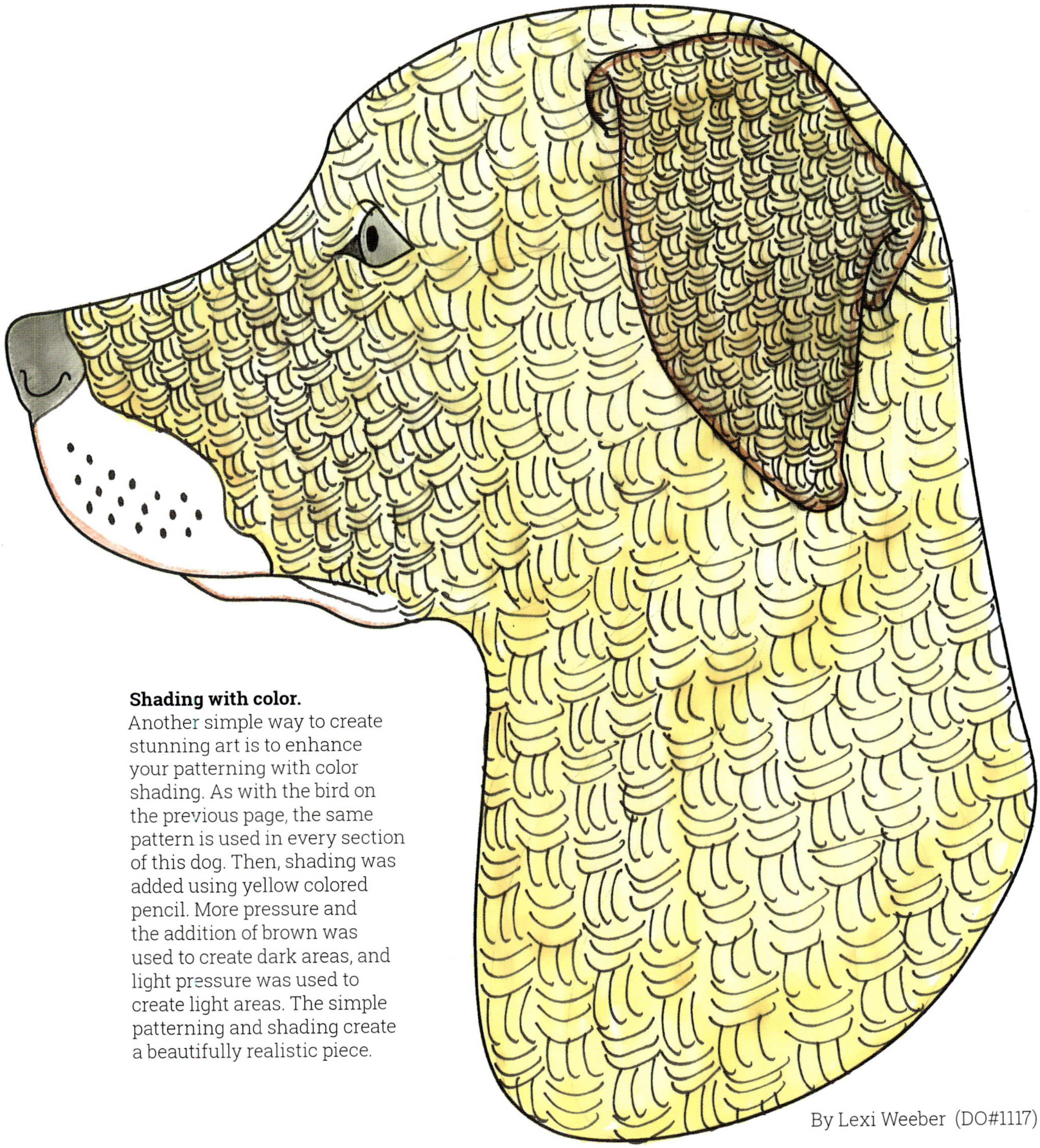

Shading with color.
Another simple way to create stunning art is to enhance your patterning with color shading. As with the bird on the previous page, the same pattern is used in every section of this dog. Then, shading was added using yellow colored pencil. More pressure and the addition of brown was used to create dark areas, and light pressure was used to create light areas. The simple patterning and shading create a beautifully realistic piece.

By Lexi Weeber (DO#1117)

Multiple patterns. As you become more comfortable with patterning, try adding a different pattern to each section of a template. This dog is filled with tangles.

Pigma Micron 01 black pens are the preferred drawing medium for tanglers. For any coloring or patterning, purchase the highest-quality supplies you can. You'll be much happier with the results.

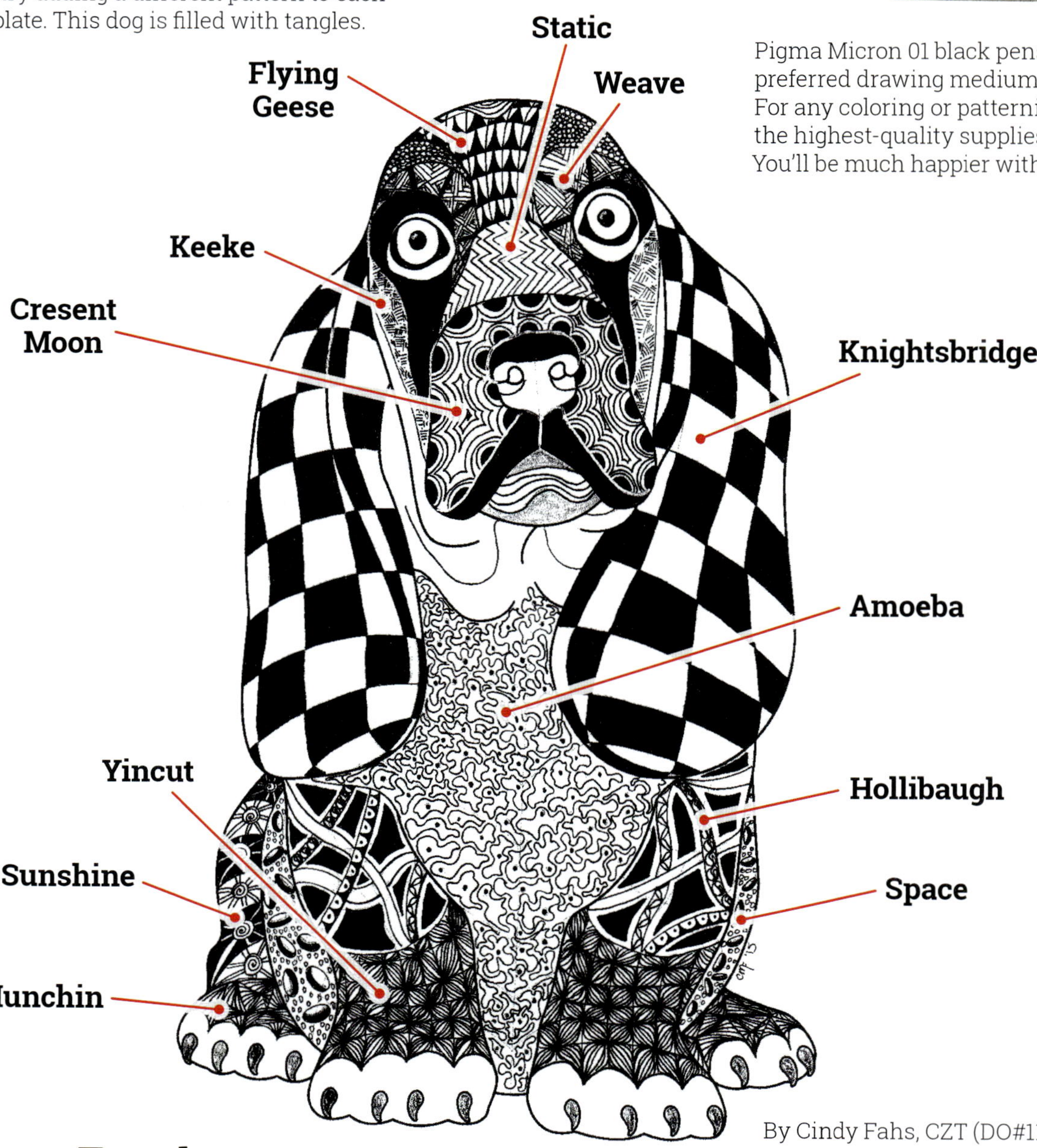

By Cindy Fahs, CZT (DO#1109)

Try These Tangles

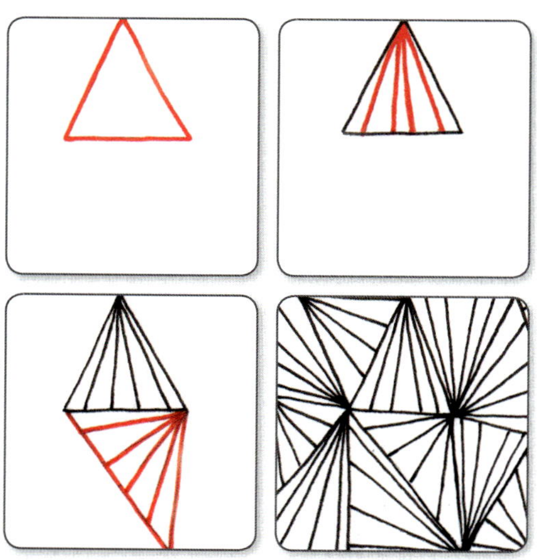

Munchin*

*An original Zentangle design

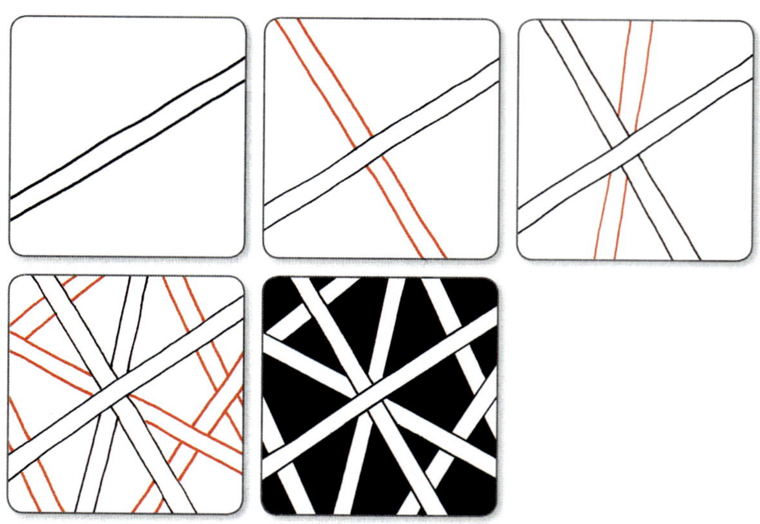

Hollibaugh*

*An original Zentangle design

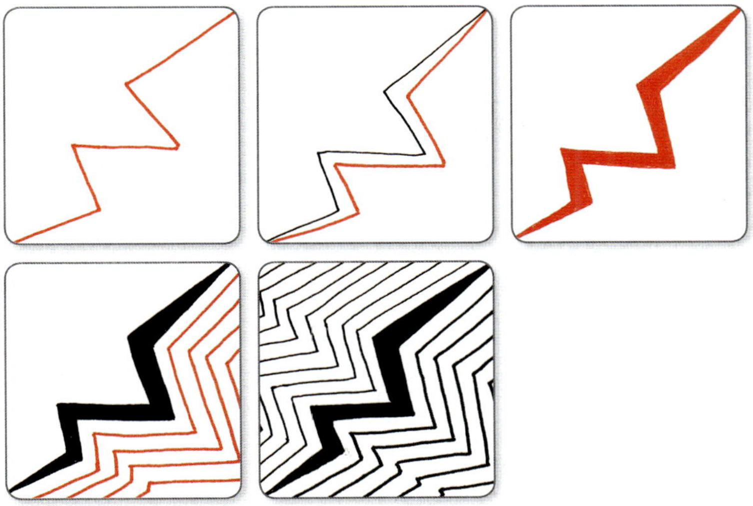

Static*

*An original Zentangle design

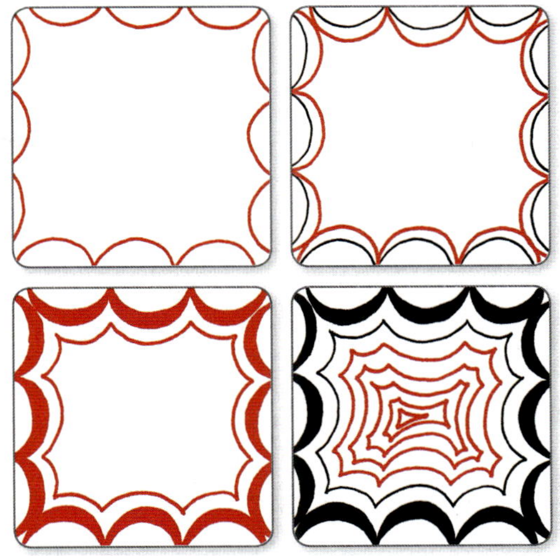

Crescent Moon*

*An original Zentangle design

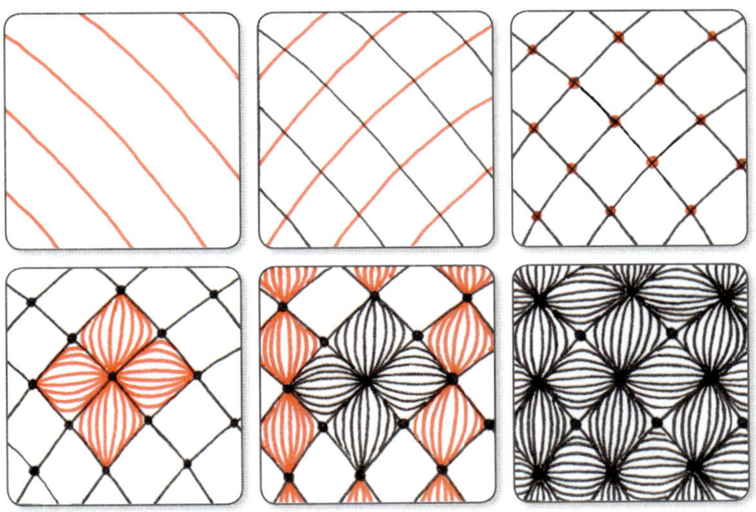

Yincut*

*An original Zentangle design

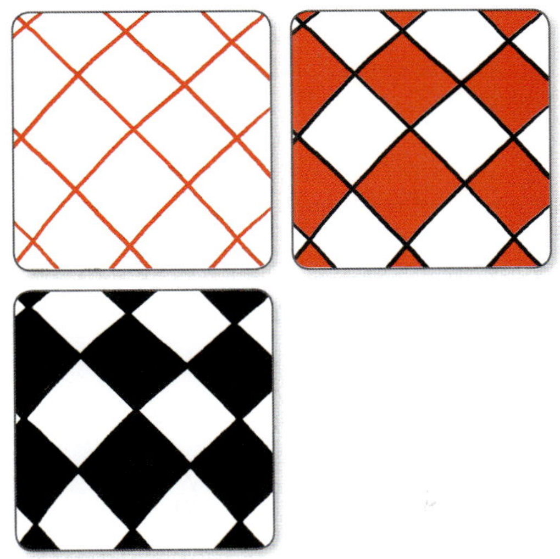

Knightsbridge*

*An original Zentangle design

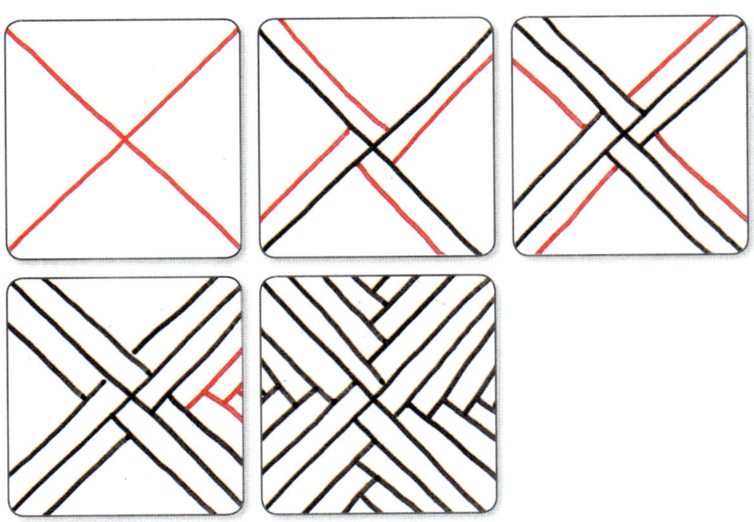

Weave

Tangle by Sandy Steen Bartholomew, CZT

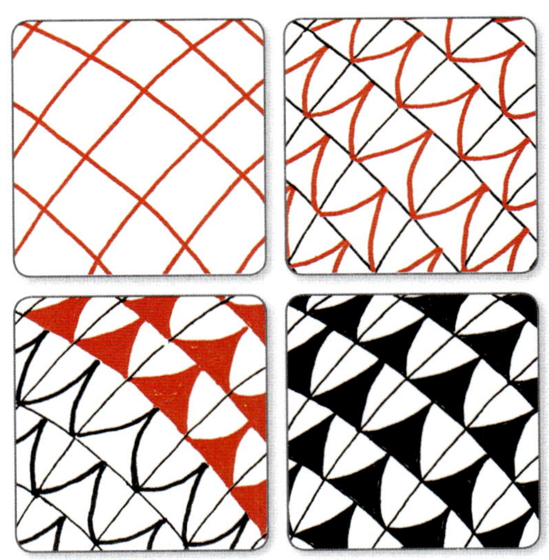

Flying Geese

Tangle by Suzanne McNeill, CZT

Design Your Own Patterns

You can also add patterning by creating your own designs using simple shapes and lines. Checkerboards, polka dots, and stripes are all patterns that anyone can draw. Check out some of the freehand patterns below to get some ideas.

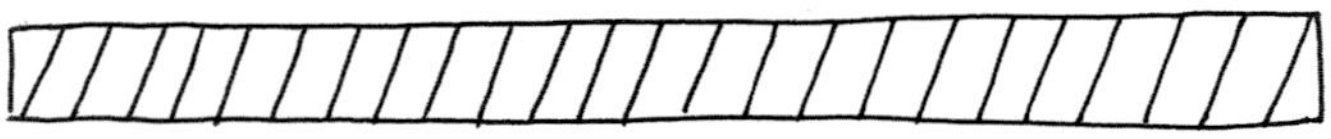

Stripes. Draw parallel lines to create stripes. You can use even spacing between the lines, or vary the spacing. Lines drawn close together will create dark areas, while lines drawn further apart will create light areas.

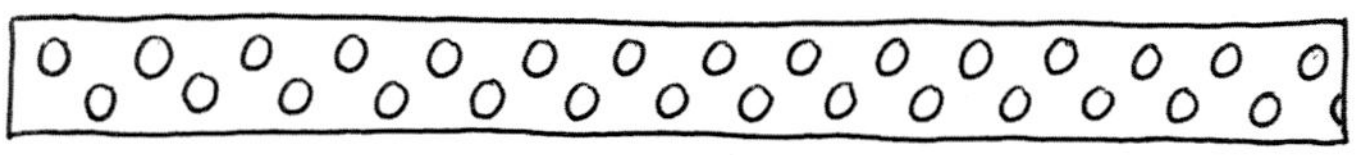

Circles. Fill a template section with circles. You can draw them in orderly rows as shown, or add them in a completely random pattern. Vary the size of the circles or keep them uniform; fill them in or leave them open; allow them to overlap or keep them separated.

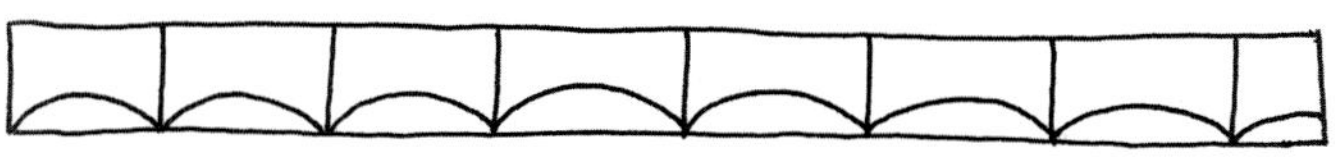

Crescents. Crescent shapes are easy to repeat along a line. Build on your design by adding more rows of crescents, or draw dots or lines between each crescent as shown.

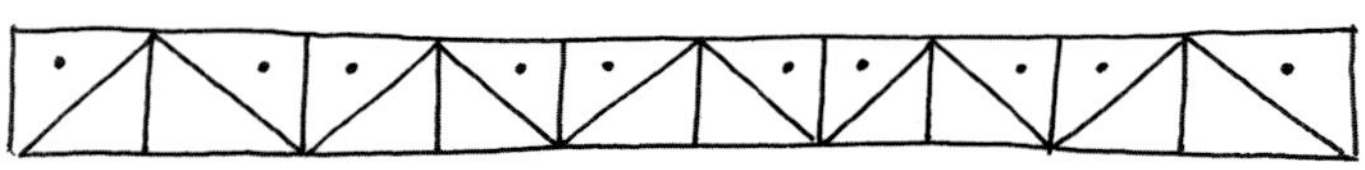

Triangles. Draw a series of triangles next to each other. Divide the triangles in half as shown, or add more lines to divide the triangles into thirds or fourths. You can also add dots and circles.

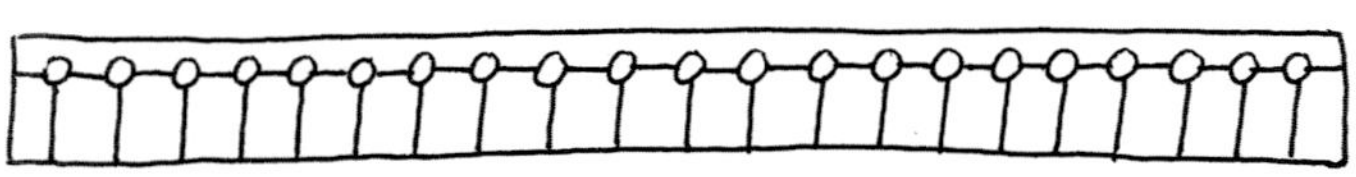

Circles and lines. Draw a series of circles. Then connect each one with a line. You can add more lines coming out from the circles. The lines can be straight and parallel, or go in any direction and crisscross.

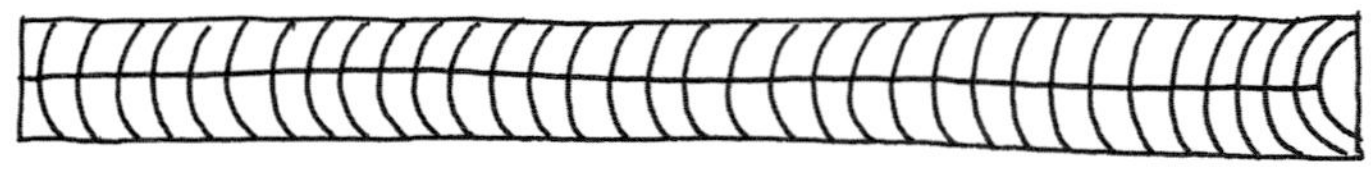

Varied stripes. You can make stripes curved or wavy for added interest. Add extra dots or lines for complexity.

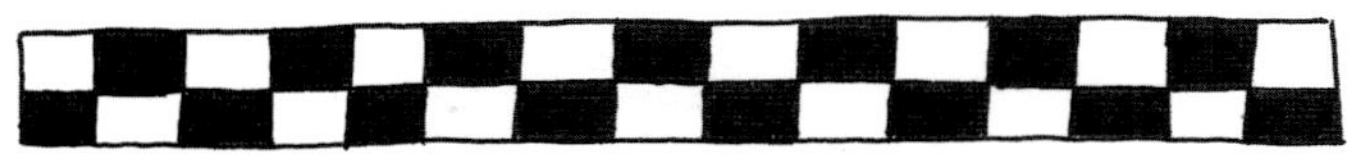

Checkerboard. Draw a grid and fill in alternating boxes for a checkerboard pattern. Use square or rectangular boxes. Or, draw a grid with curved lines for added interest.

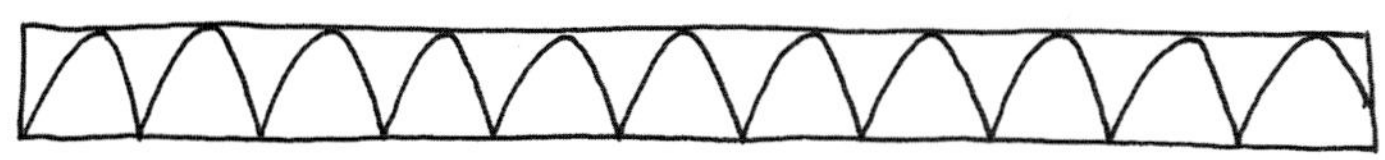

Extended crescents. These tall crescents make a great border around the edges of a section in a template.

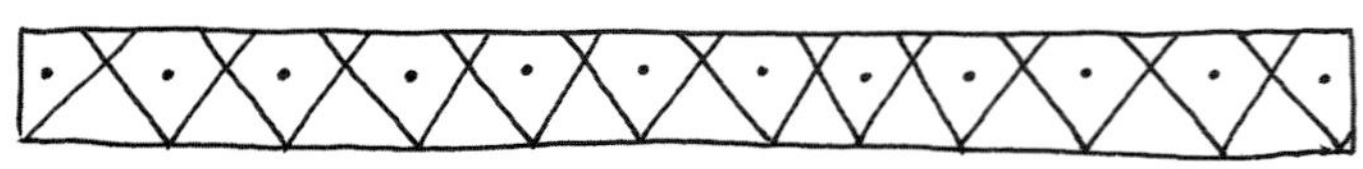

Overlapping triangles. Draw a series of triangles so that they overlap. Add extra lines and dots for complexity.

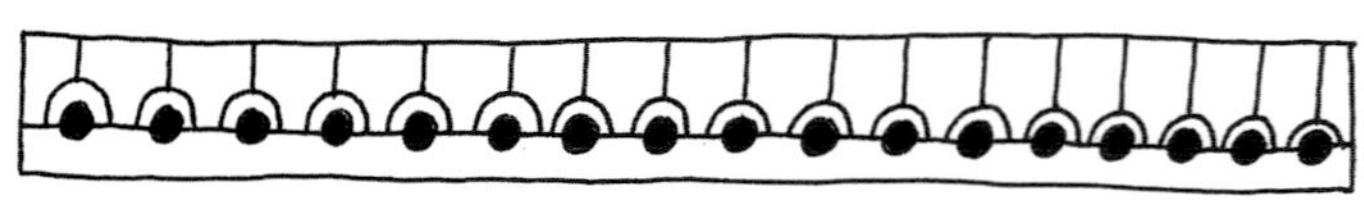

Varied circles and lines. Add more complexity to the circles and lines design by filling in the circles and adding semi-circle outlines.

Inspirational Gallery

We asked people to share the amazing art they've been creating using the templates found in this book. We've featured their beautiful work here to spark your creativity and get ready to create some art of your own. Notice how the same template can look completely different depending on the way each artist used the guidelines and the patterns or colors added. Remember to put your individual touch and style on every piece you create. Have fun!

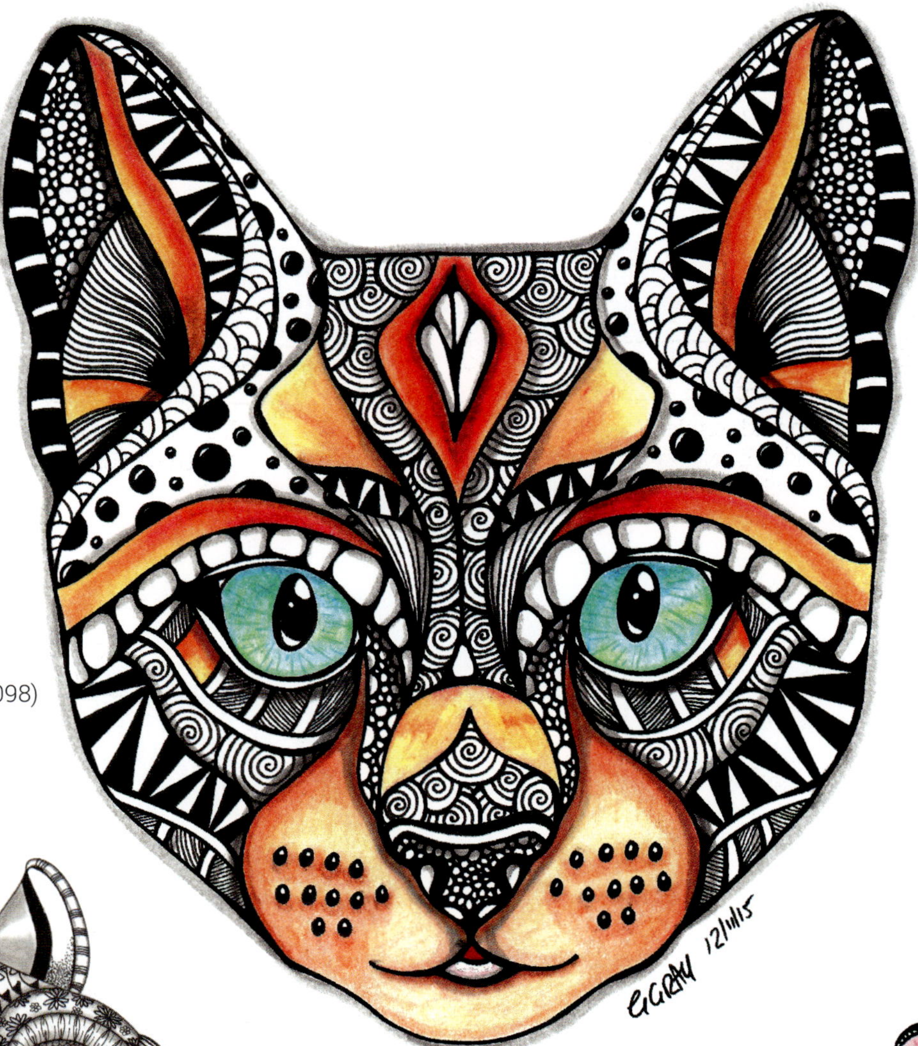

By Abbey Gray (DO#1098)

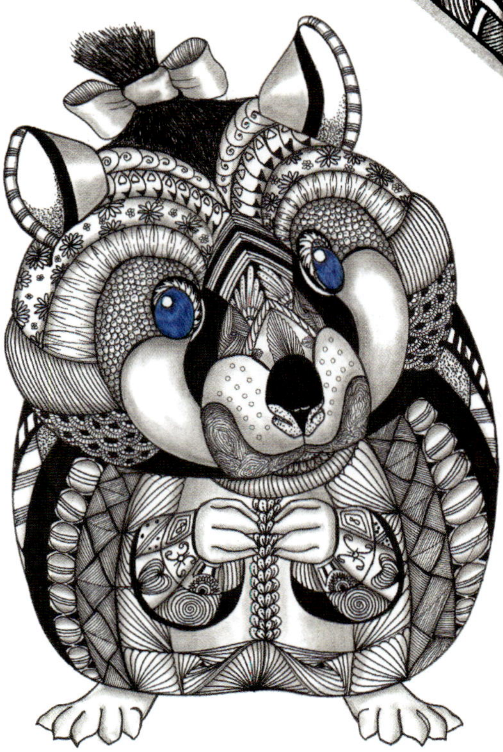

By Elaine Sampson (DO#1107)

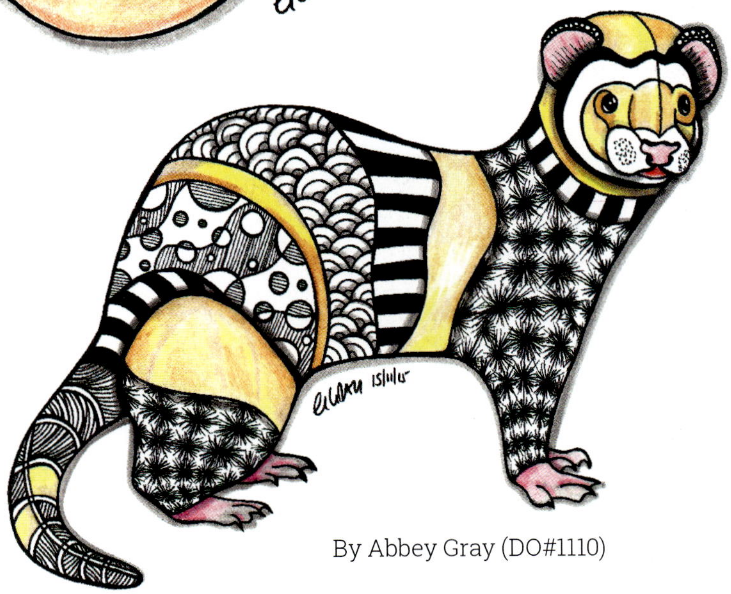

By Abbey Gray (DO#1110)

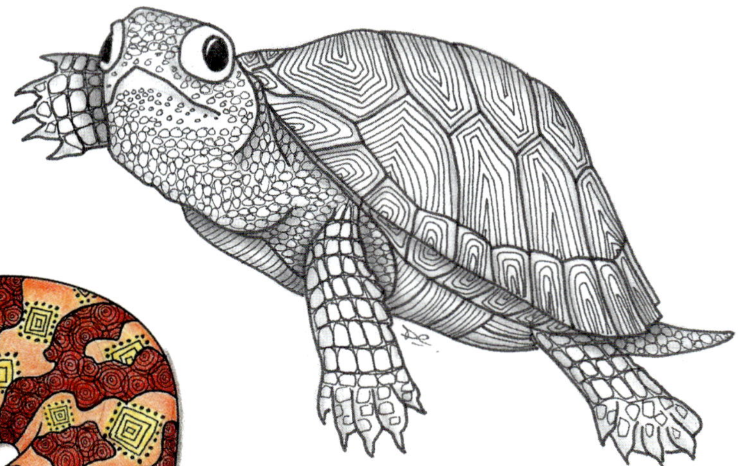

By Dawn Collins (DO#1116)

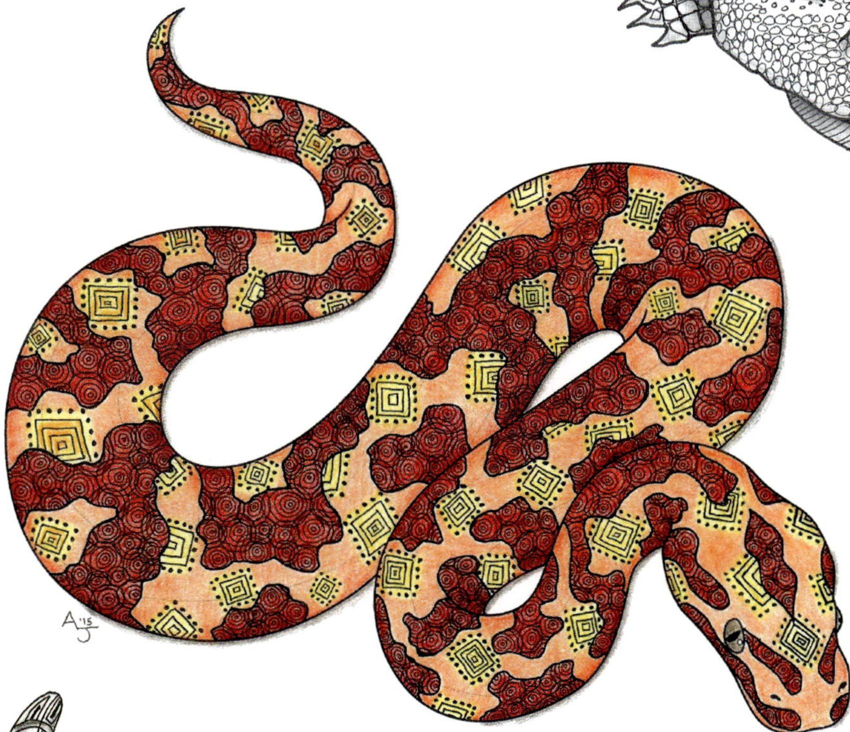

By Annie Jump (DO#1097)

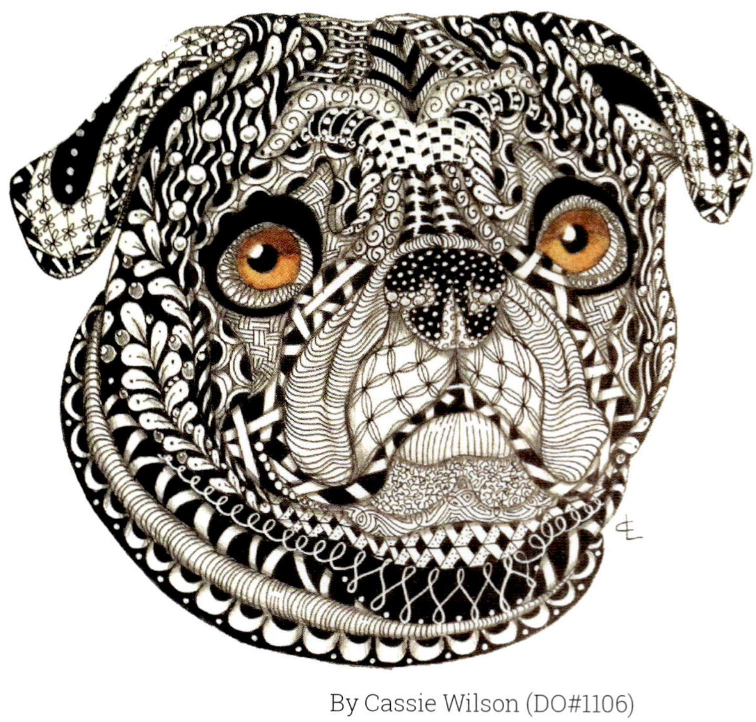

By Cassie Wilson (DO#1106)

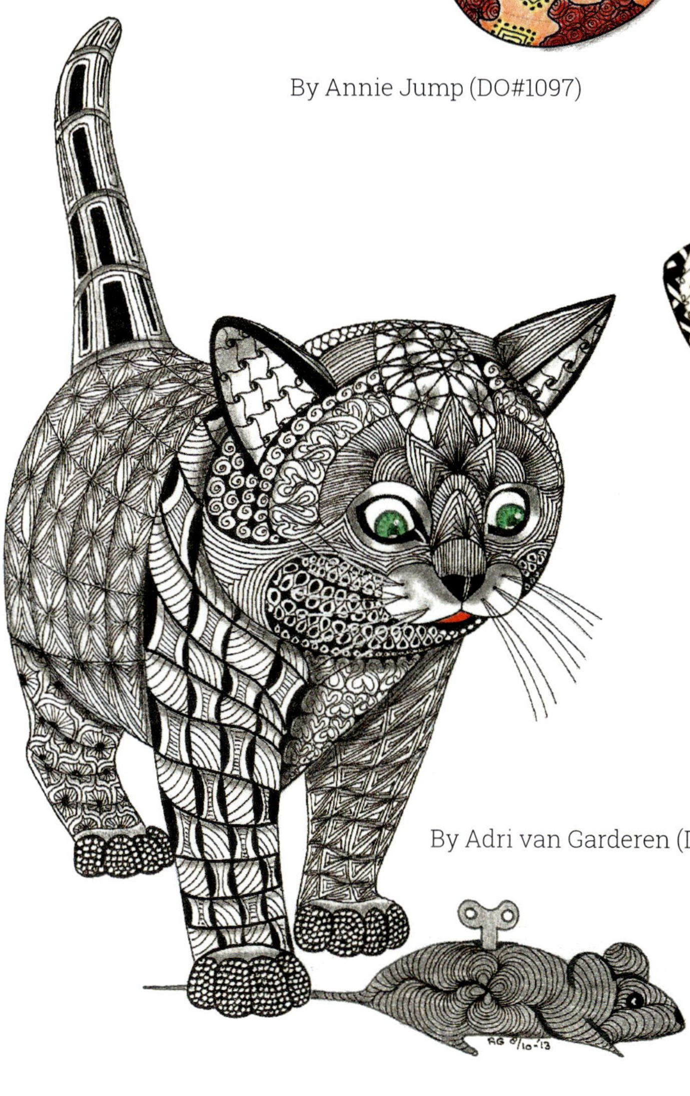

By Adri van Garderen (DO#1094)

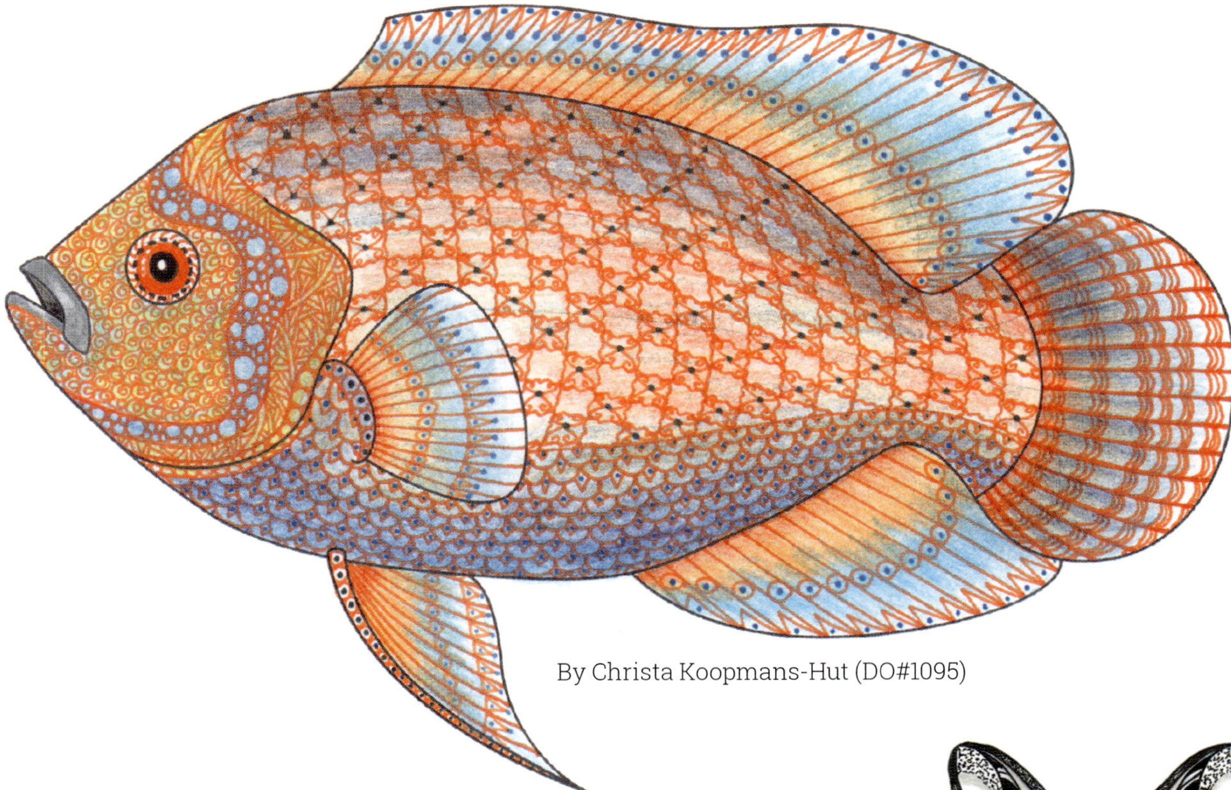

By Christa Koopmans-Hut (DO#1095)

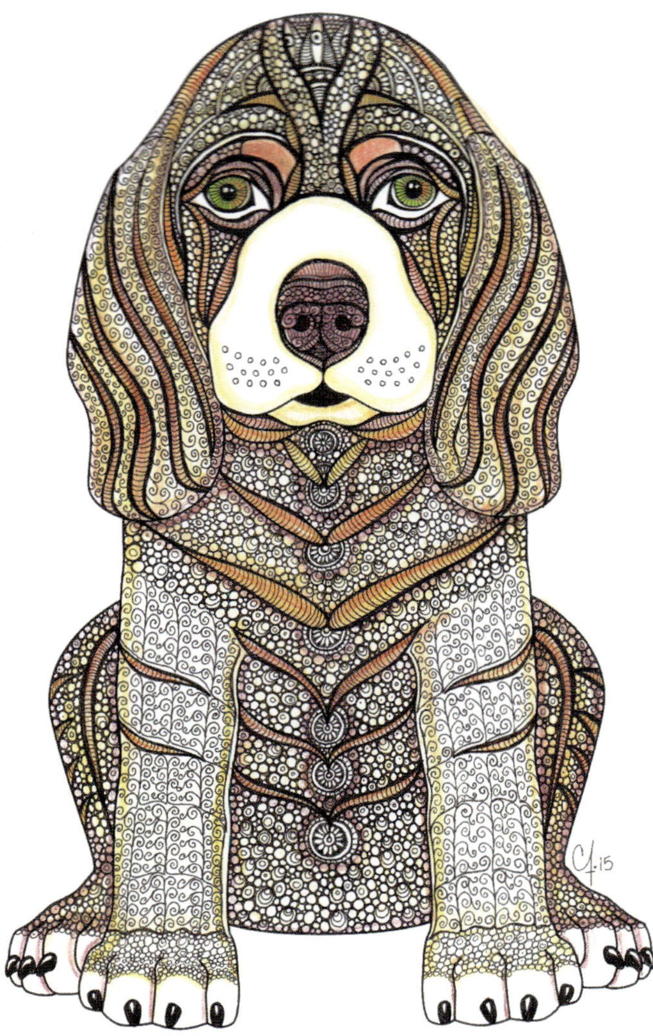

By Candice Ferguson (DO#1102)

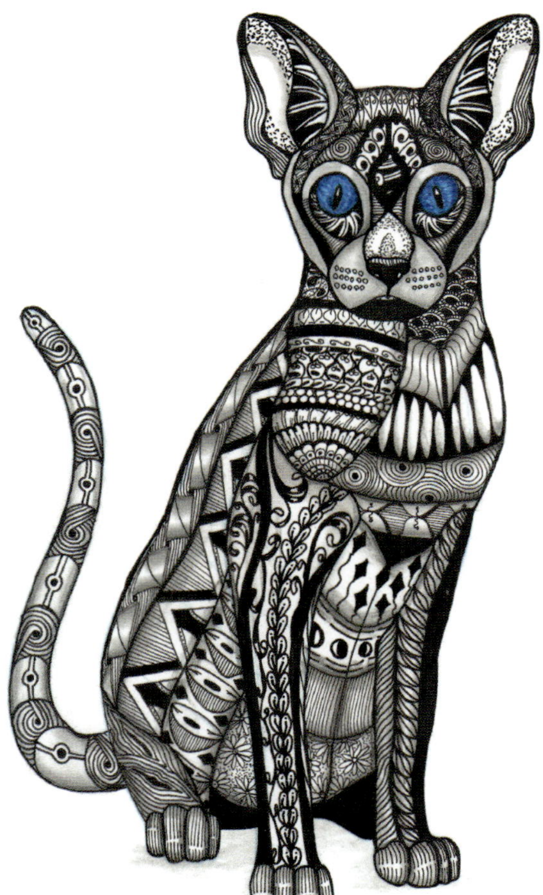

By Elaine Sampson (DO#1105)

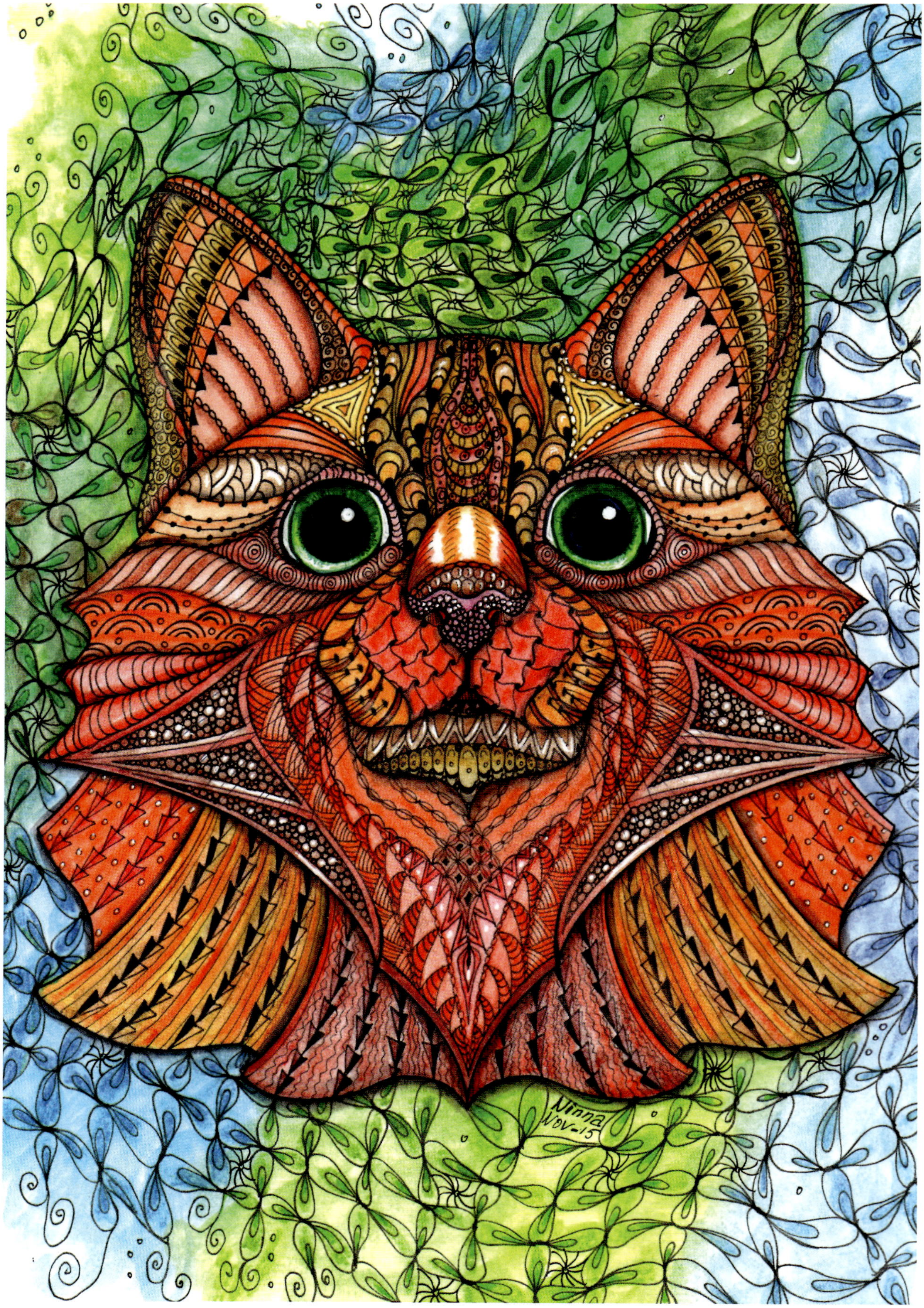

By Ninna Hellman (DO#1114)

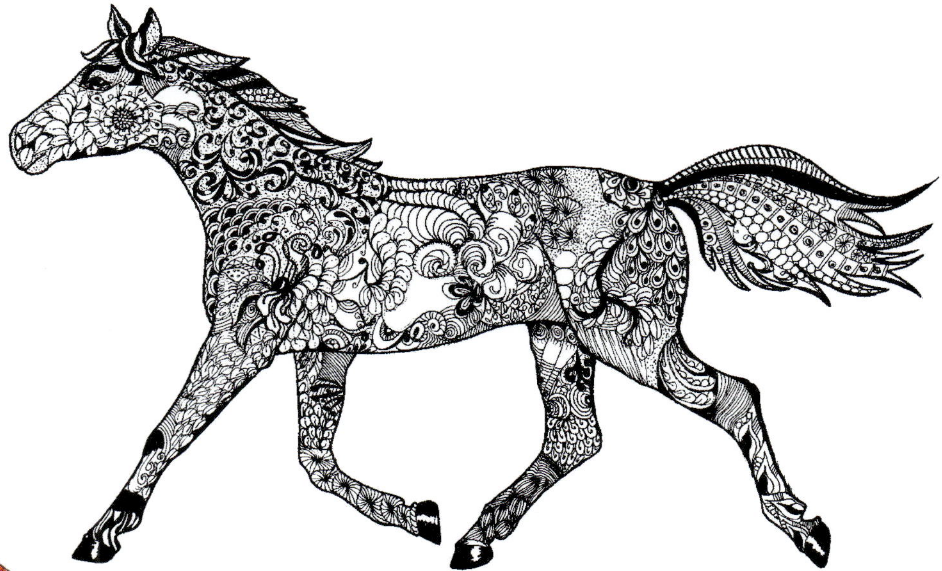

By Elaine Sampson (DO#1103)

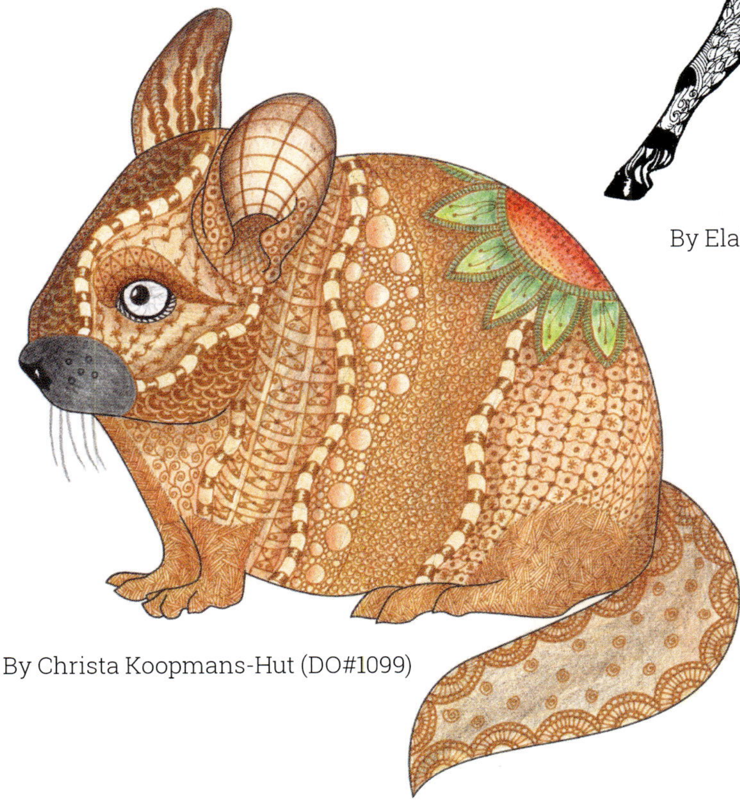

By Christa Koopmans-Hut (DO#1099)

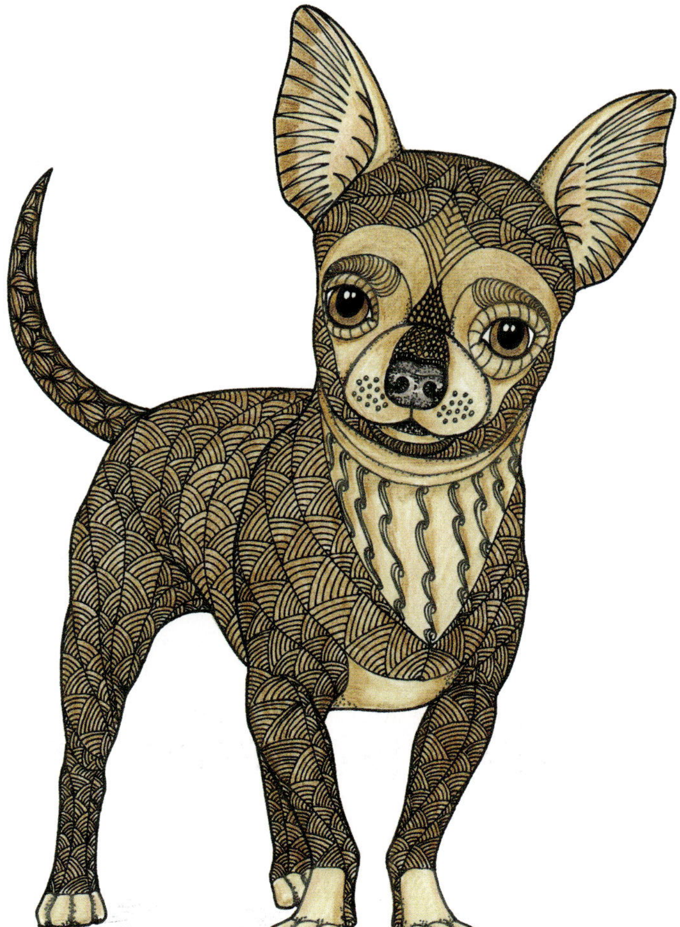

By Darla Tjelmeland (DO#1096)

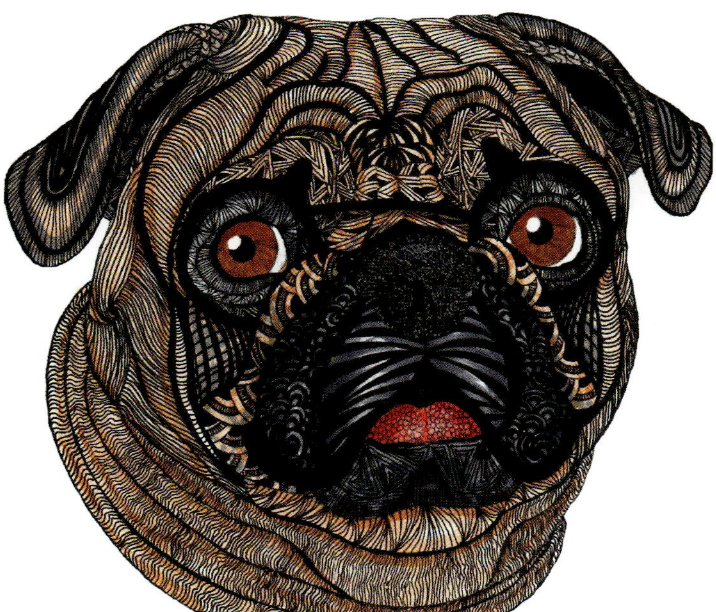

By Linda McMillen (DO#1106)

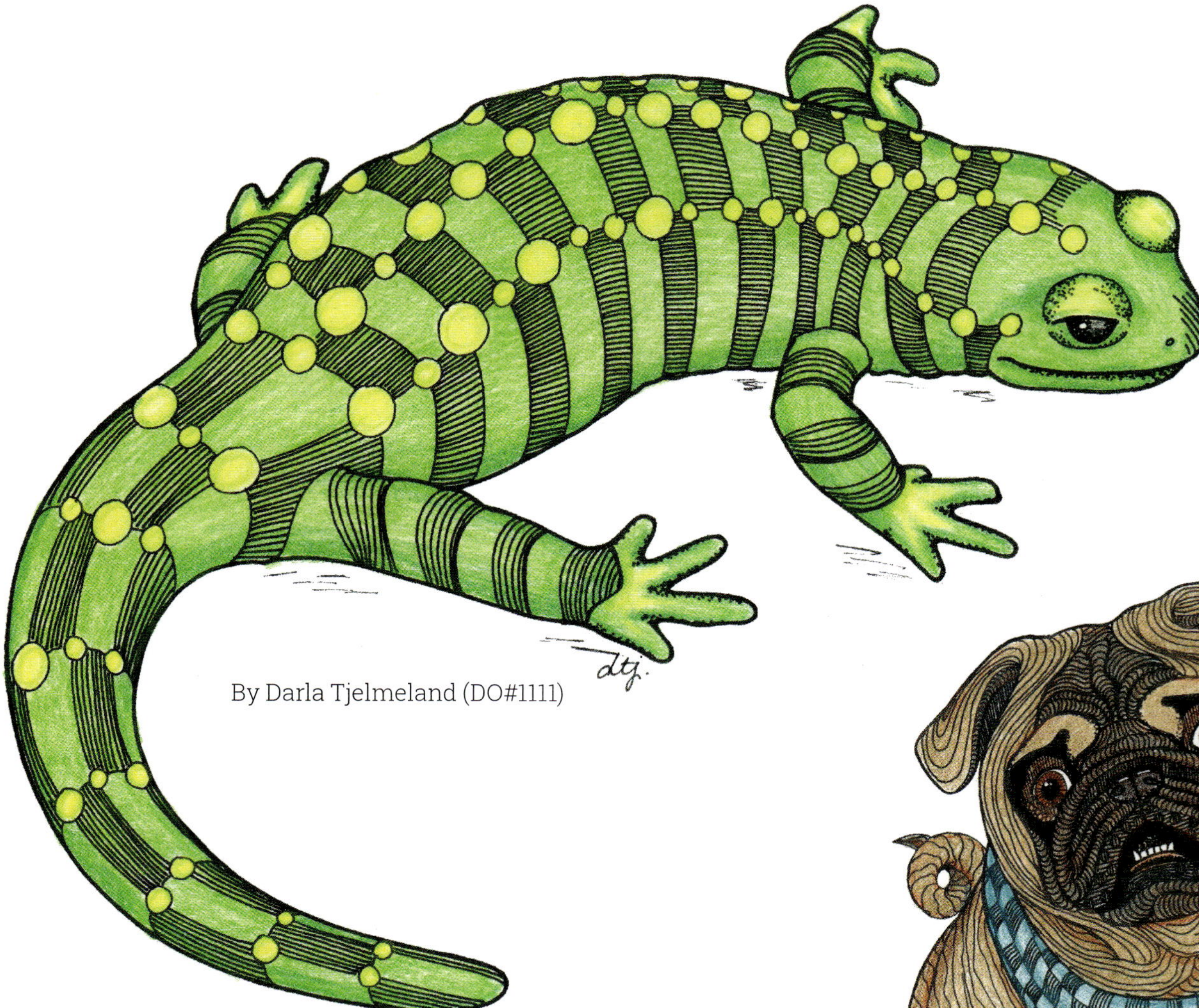

By Darla Tjelmeland (DO#1111)

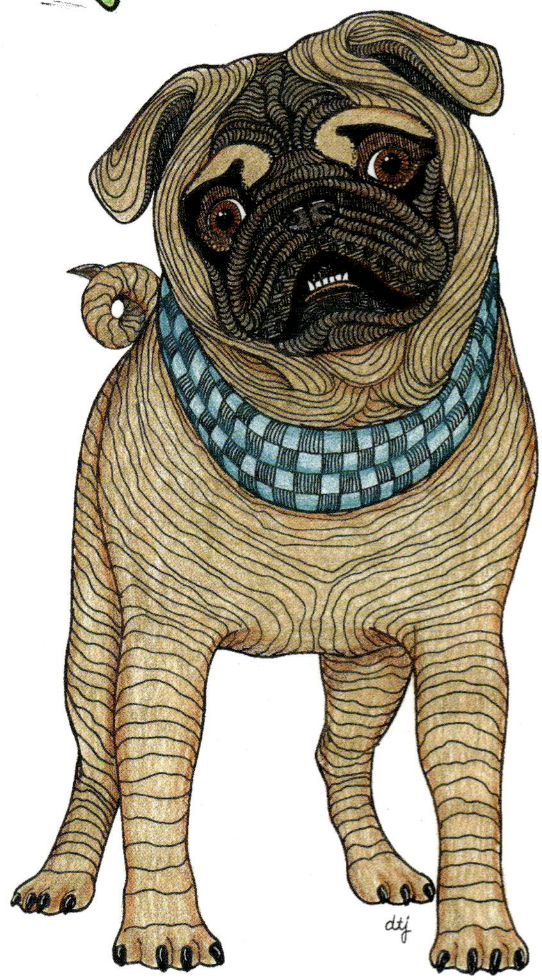

By Darla Tjelmeland (DO#1122)

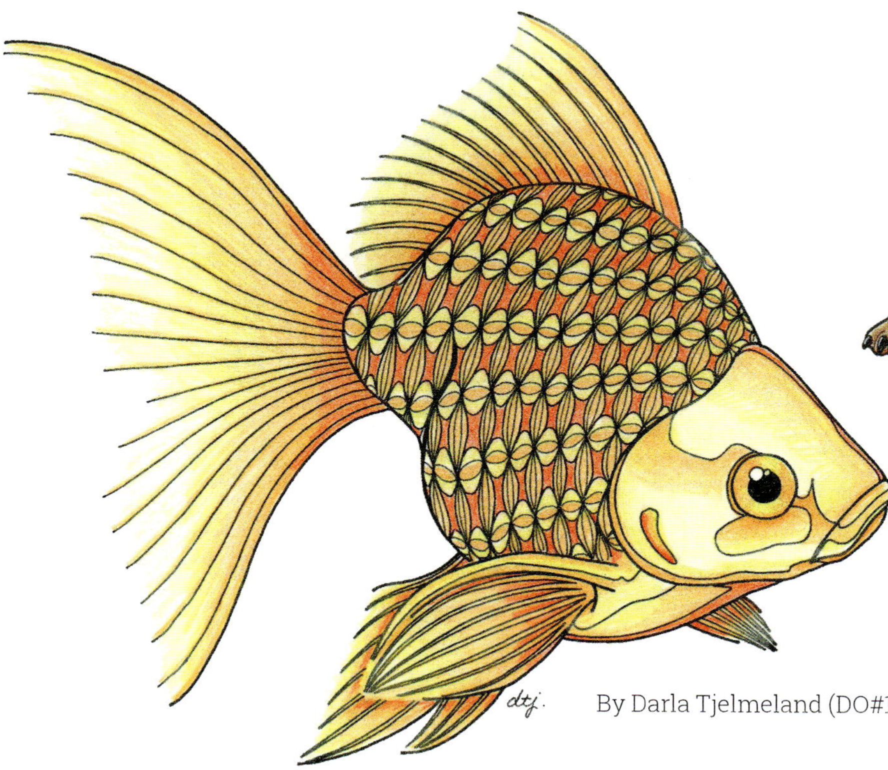

By Darla Tjelmeland (DO#1118)

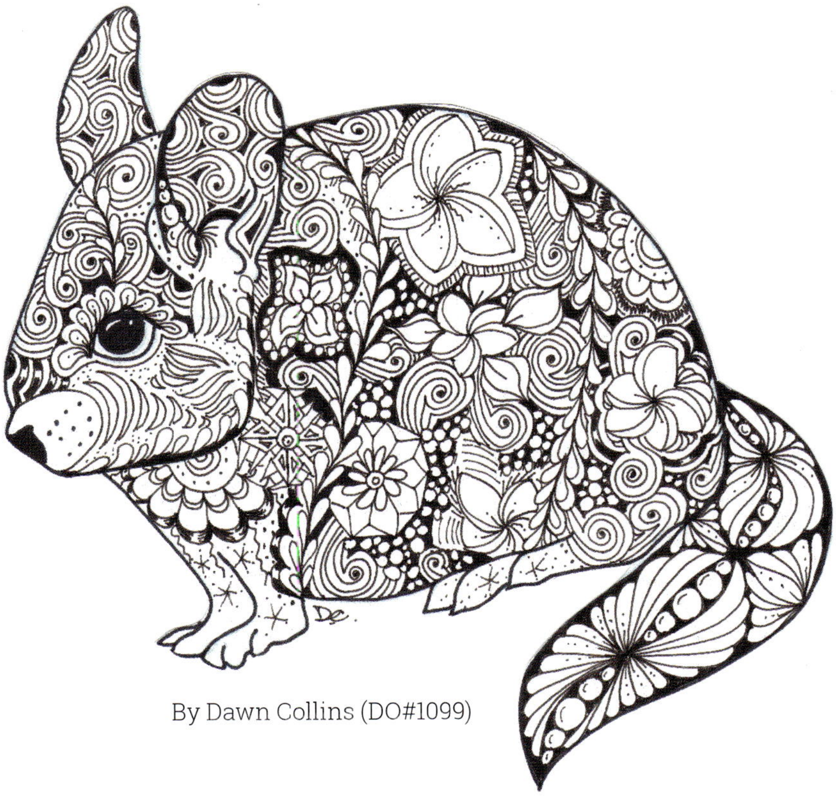

By Dawn Collins (DO#1099)

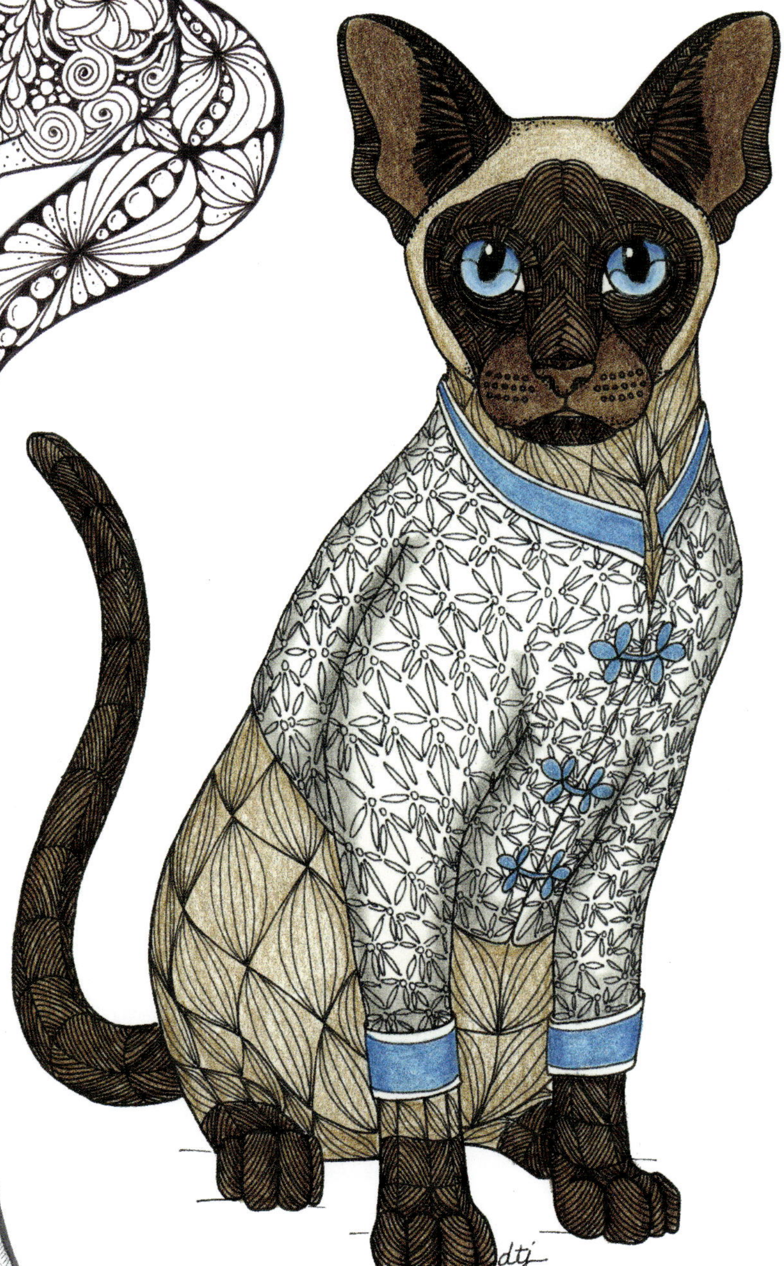

By Darla Tjelmeland (DO#1105)

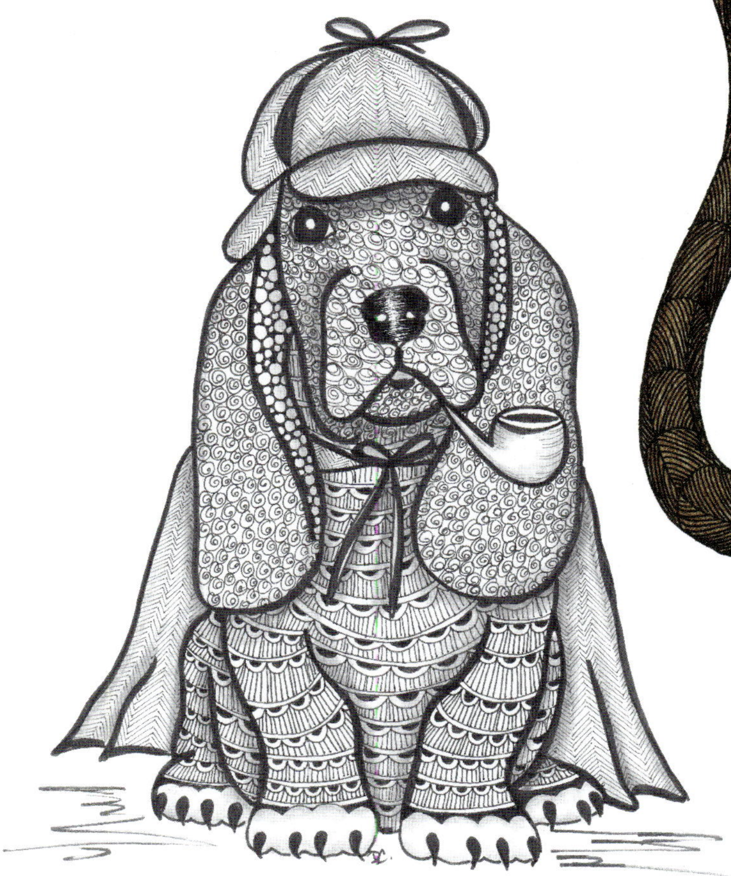

By Dawn Collins (DO#1109)

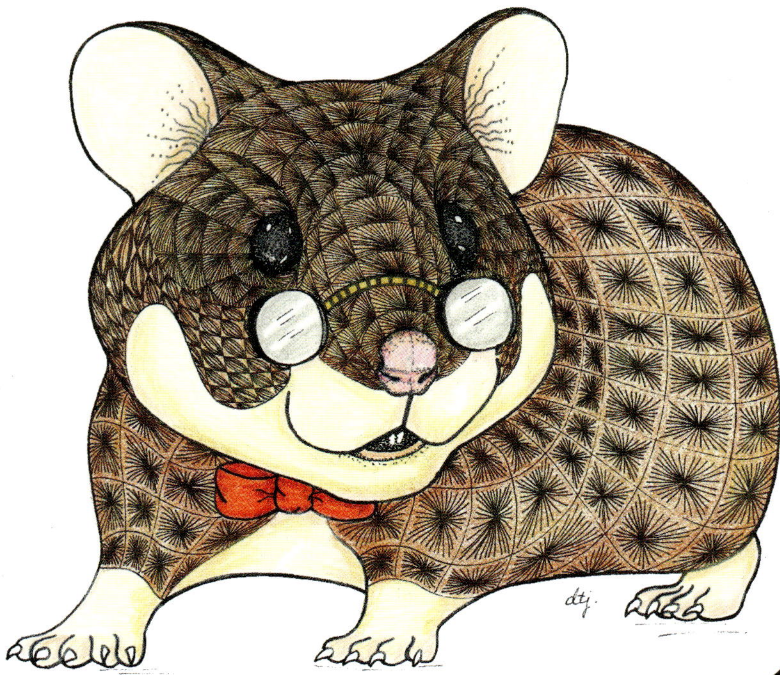

By Darla Tjelmeland (DO#1093)

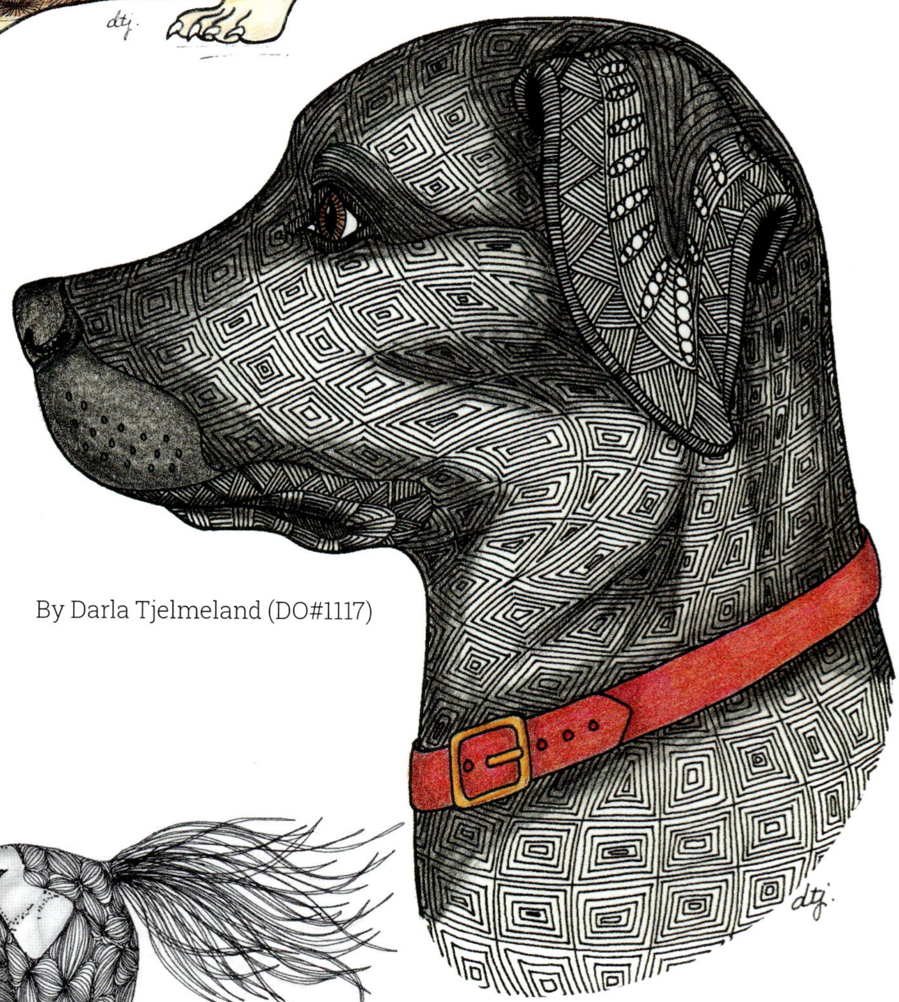

By Darla Tjelmeland (DO#1117)

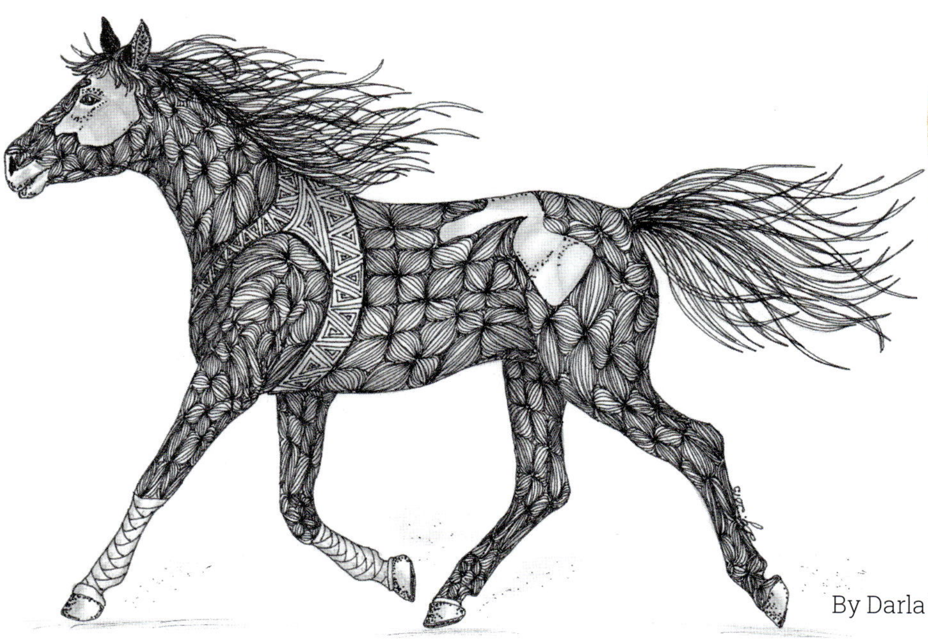

By Darla Tjelmeland (DO#1103)

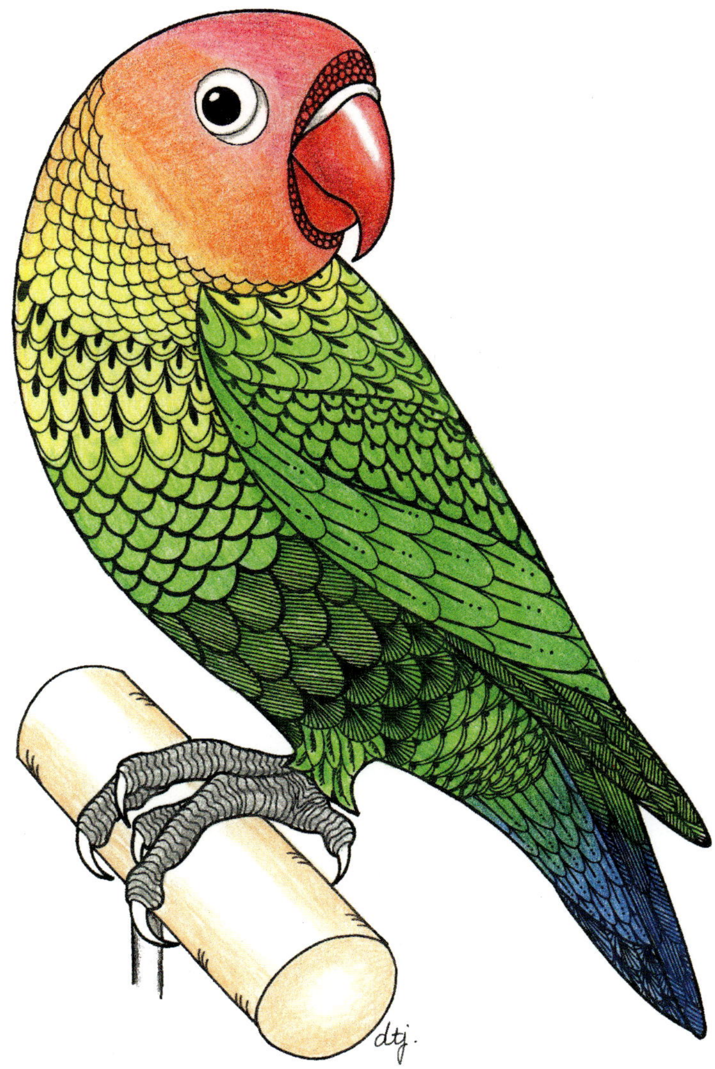

By Darla Tjelmeland (DO#1112)

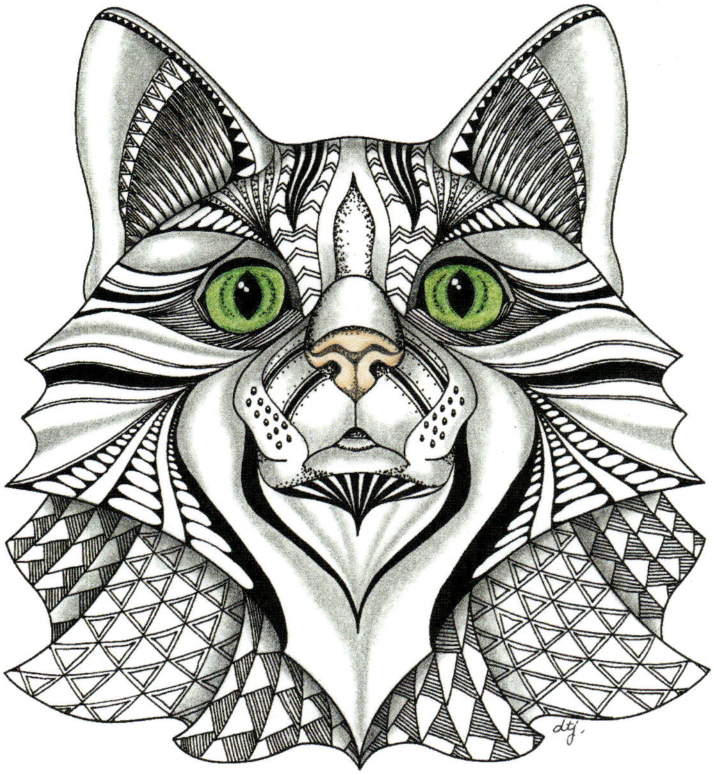

By Darla Tjelmeland (DO#1114)

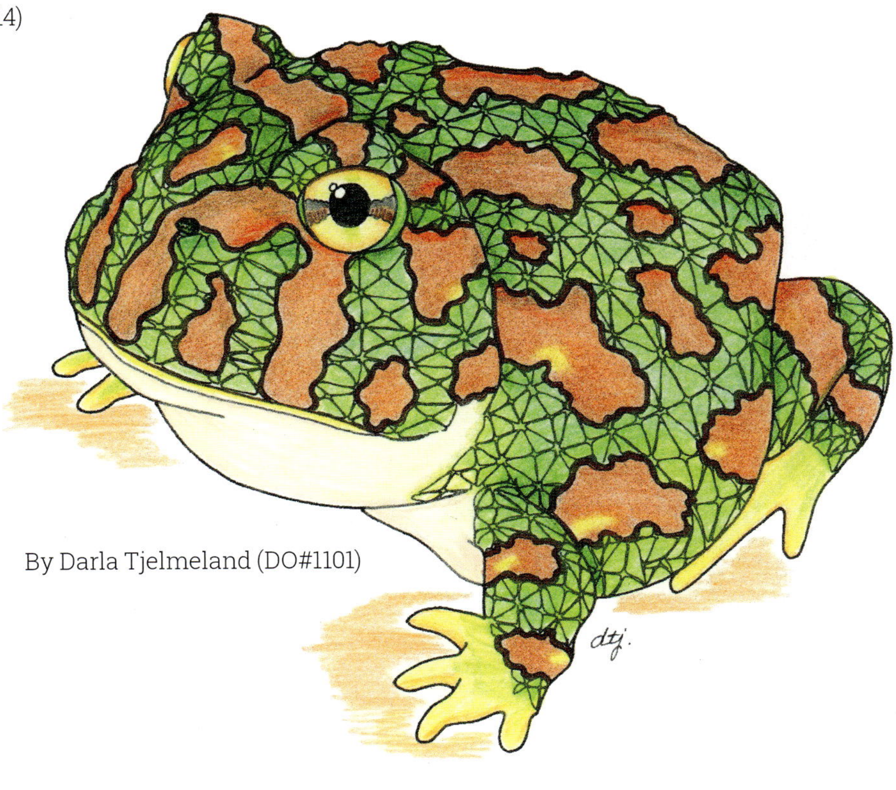

By Darla Tjelmeland (DO#1101)

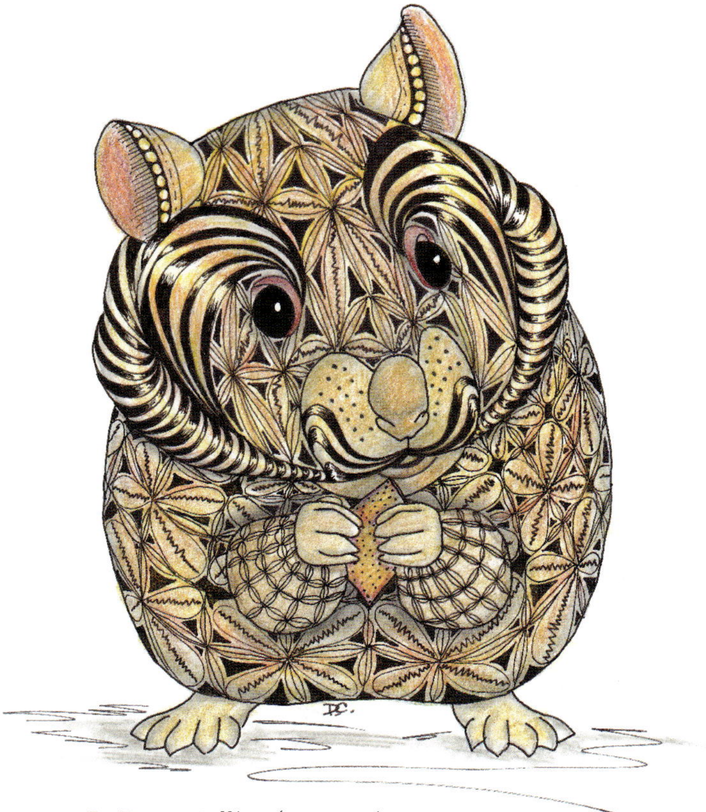

By Dawn Collins (DO#1107)

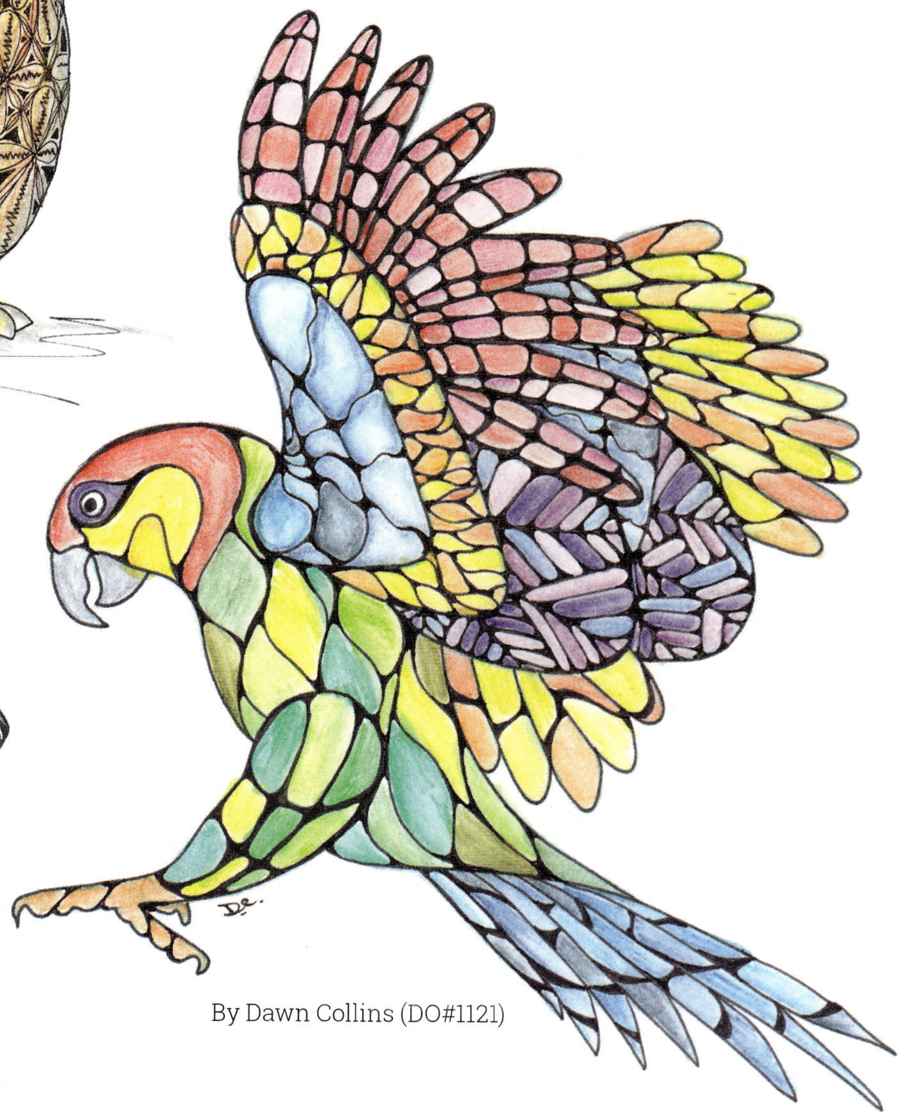

By Dawn Collins (DO#1121)

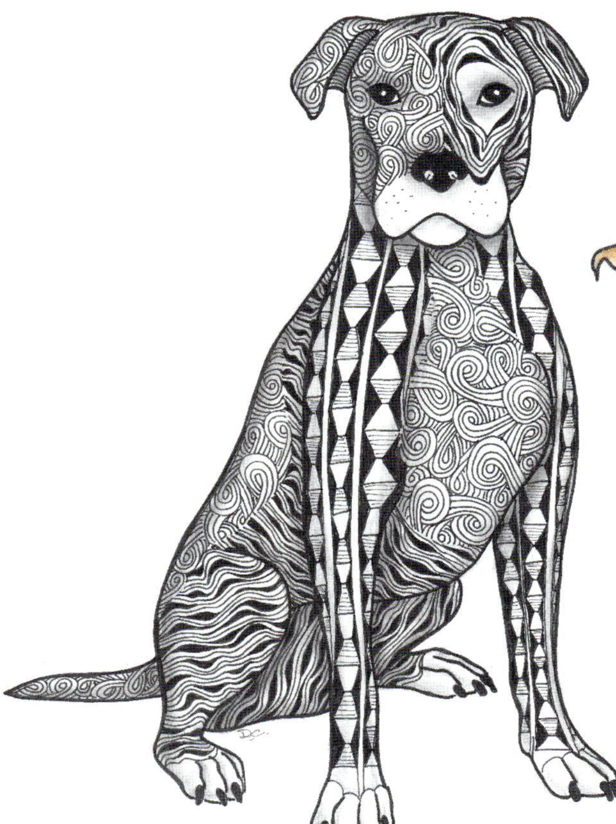

By Dawn Collins (DO#1100)

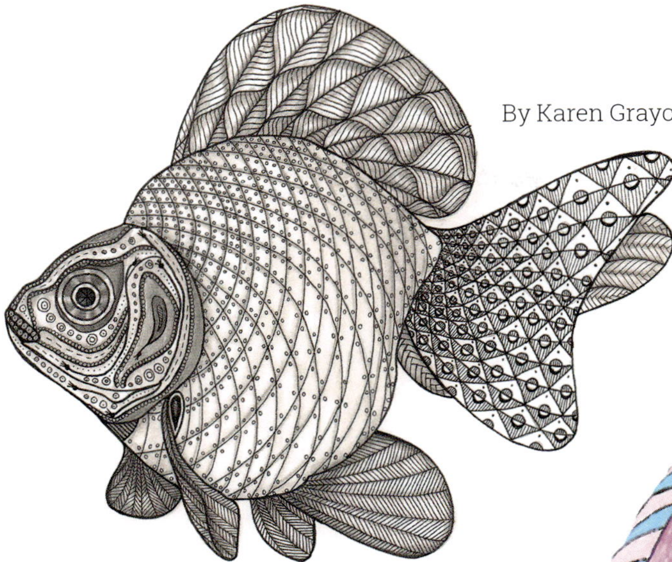

By Karen Grayczk (DO#1118)

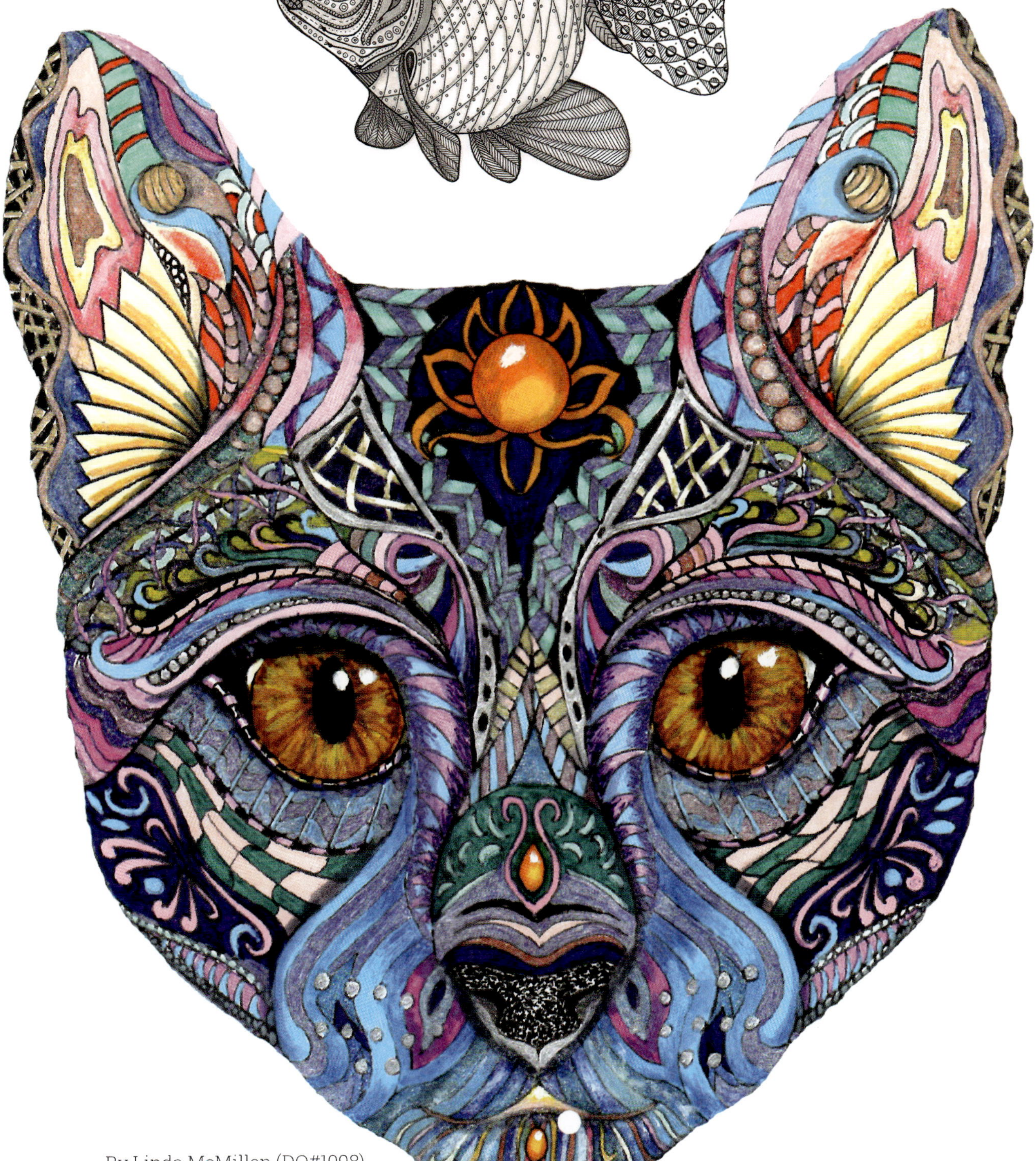

By Linda McMillen (DO#1098)

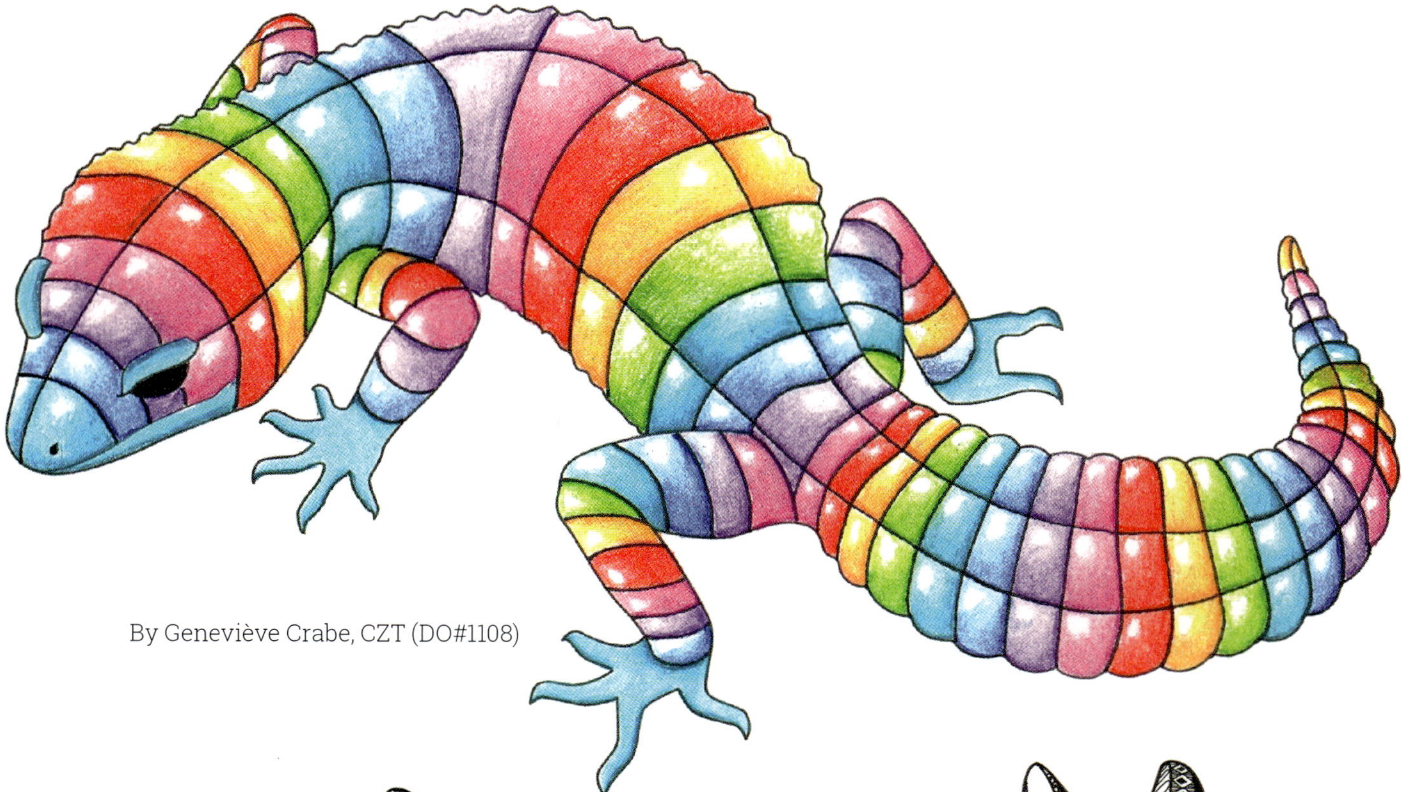

By Geneviève Crabe, CZT (DO#1108)

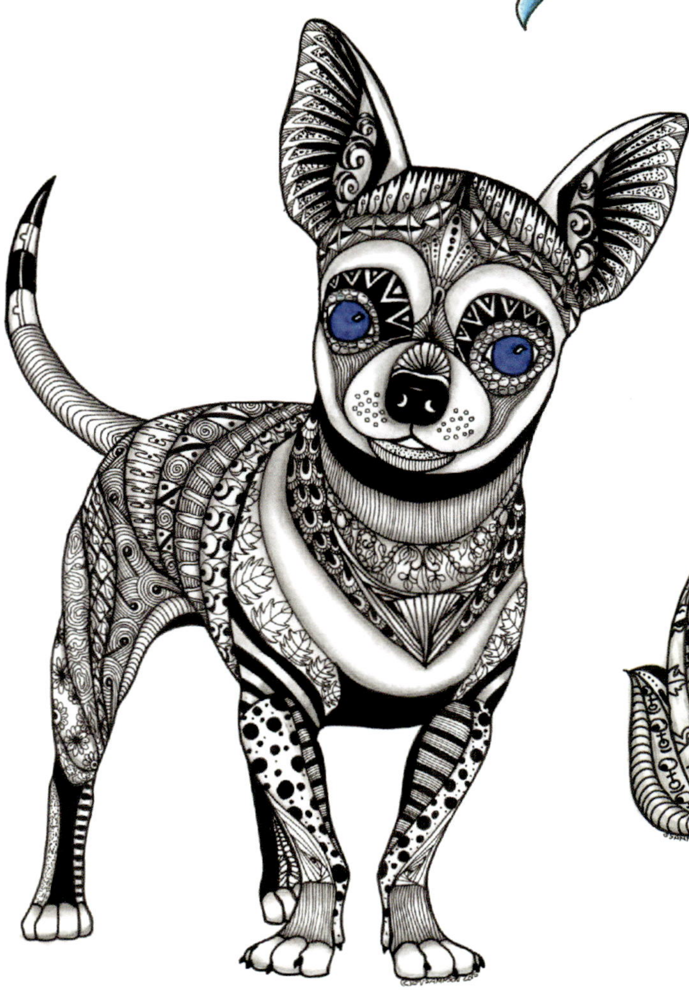

By Elaine Sampson (DO#1096)

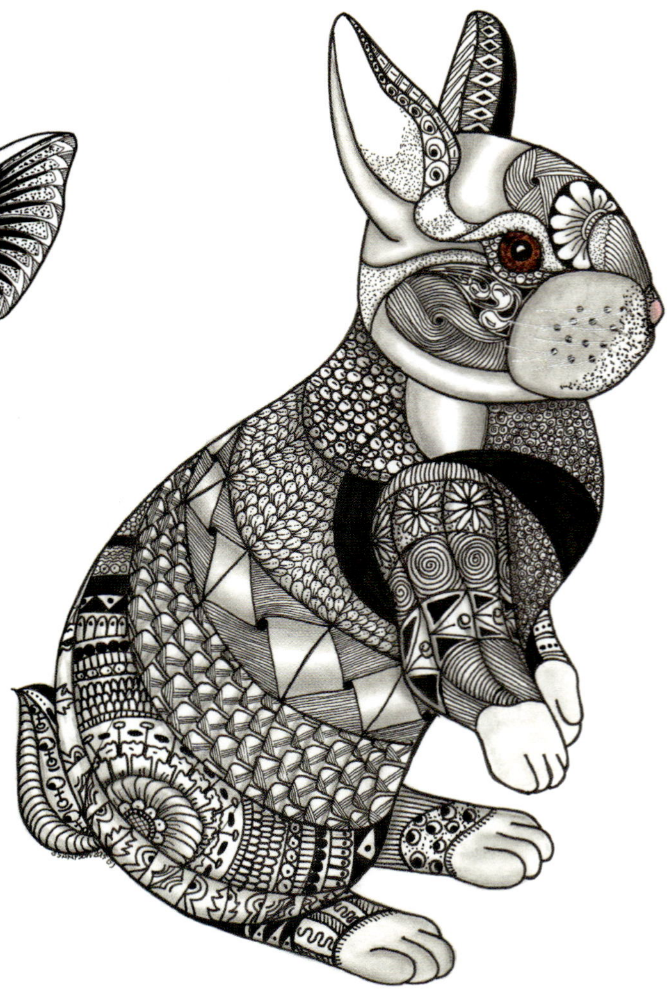

By Elaine Sampson (DO#1120)

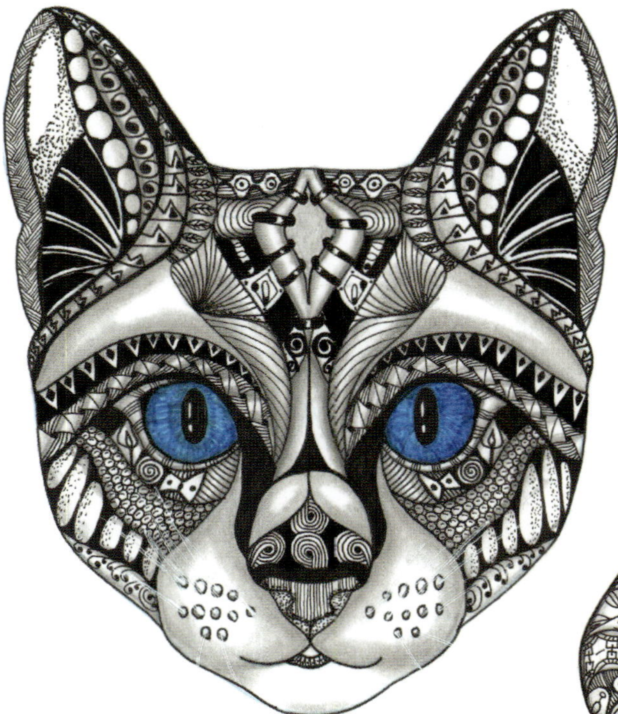

By Elaine Sampson (DO#1098)

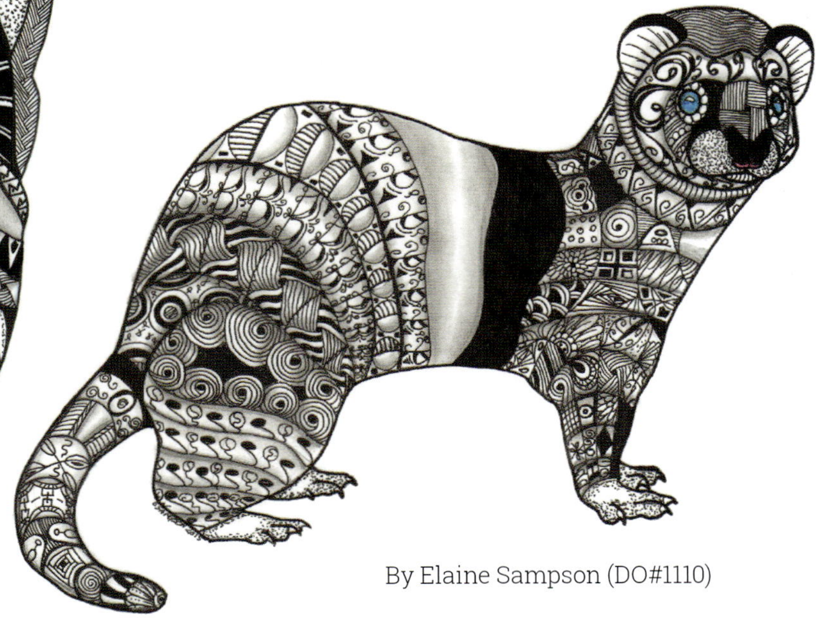

By Elaine Sampson (DO#1110)

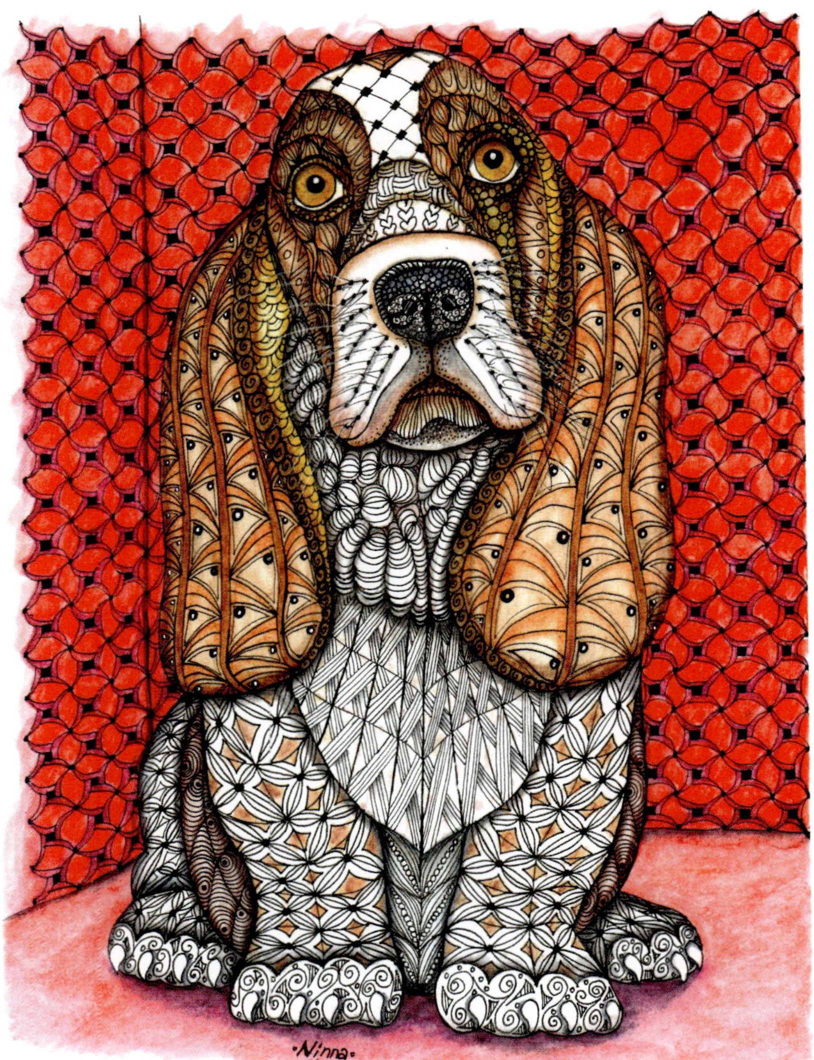

By Ninna Hellman (DO#1109)

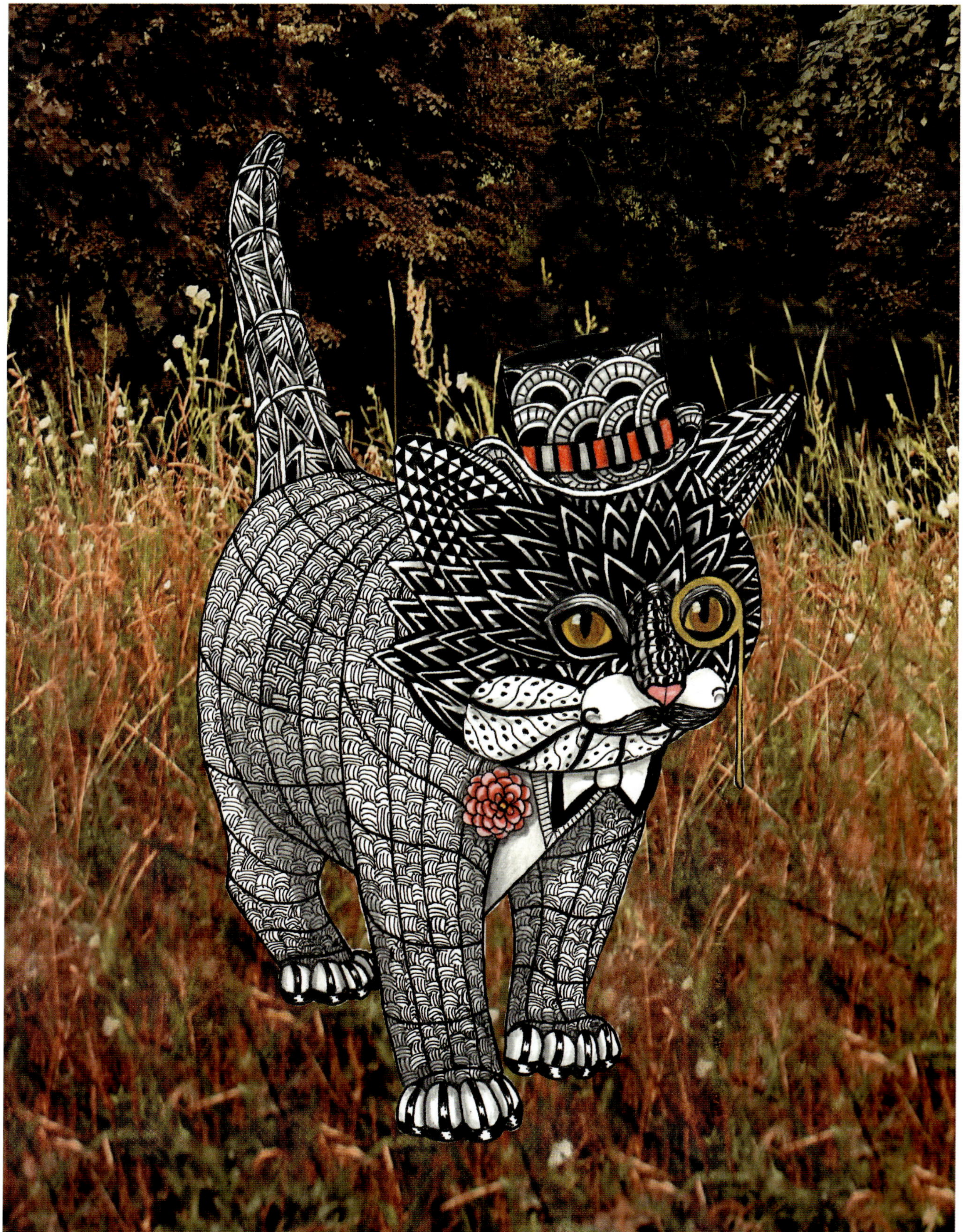

By Linda McMillen (DO#1094)

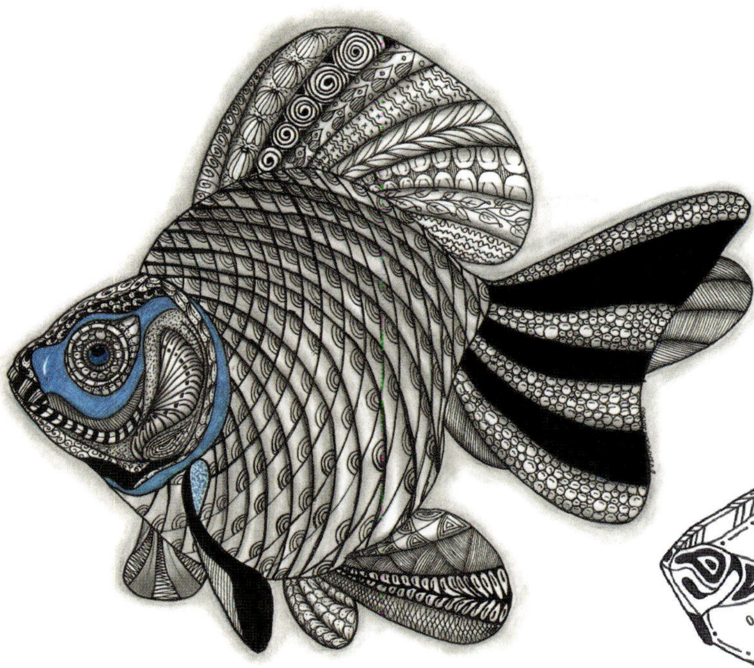

By Elaine Sampson (DO#1118)

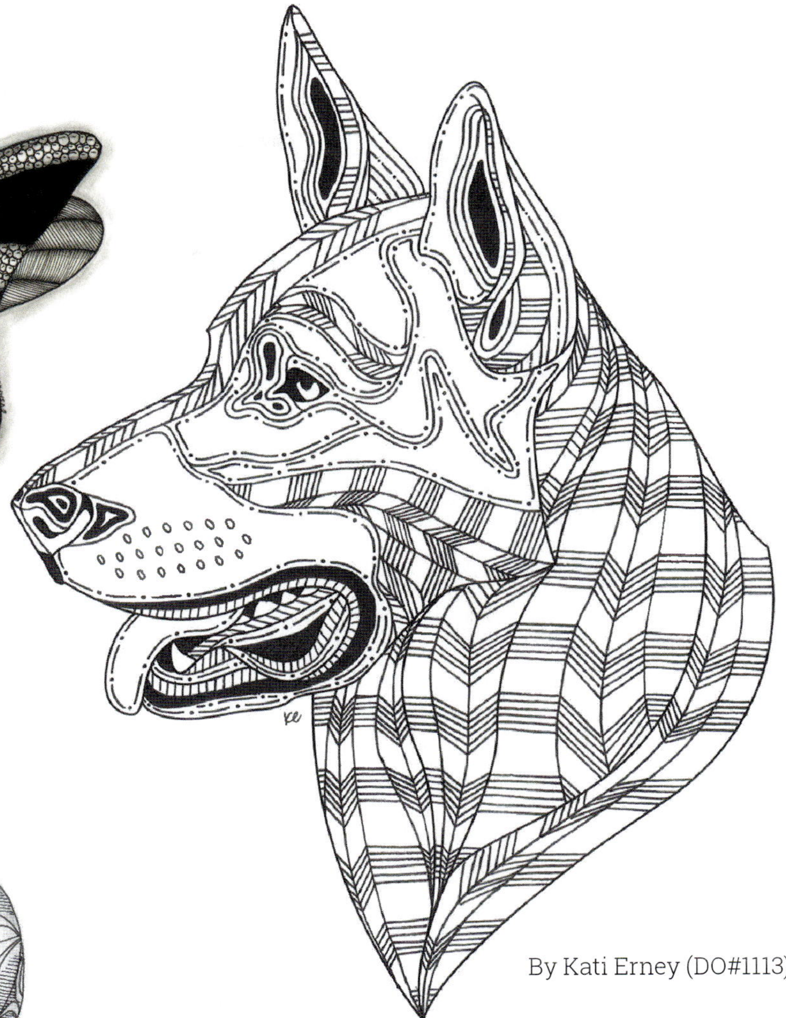

By Kati Erney (DO#1113)

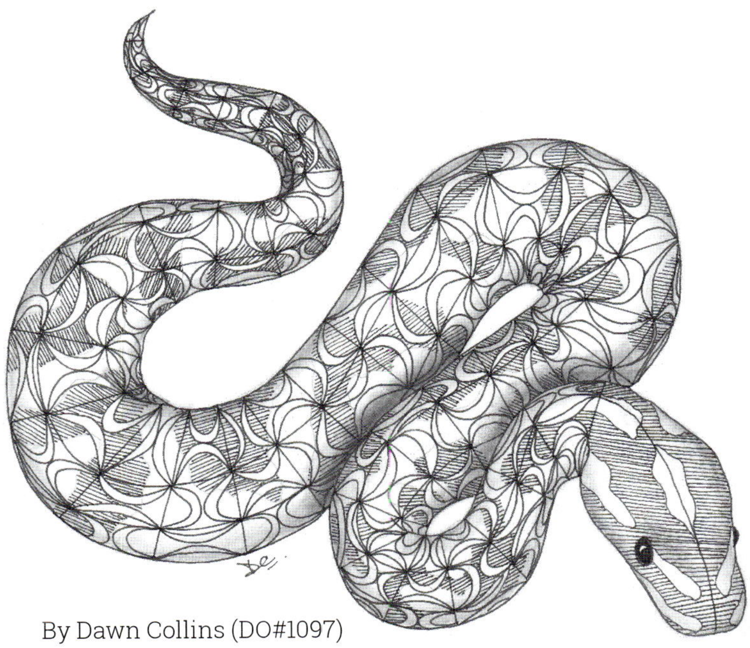

By Dawn Collins (DO#1097)

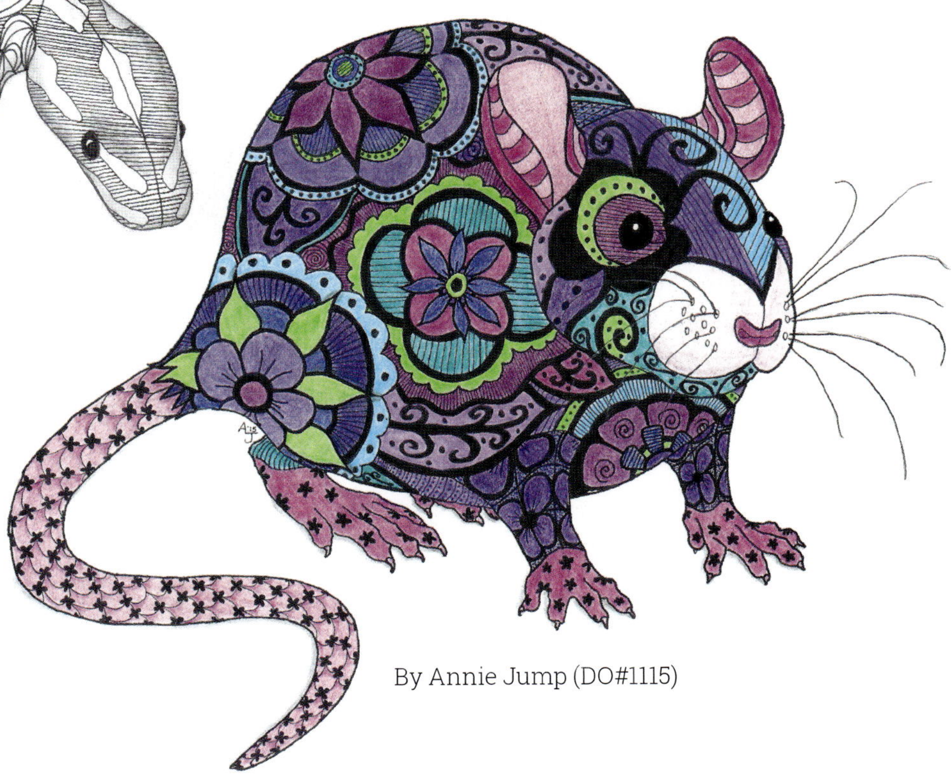

By Annie Jump (DO#1115)

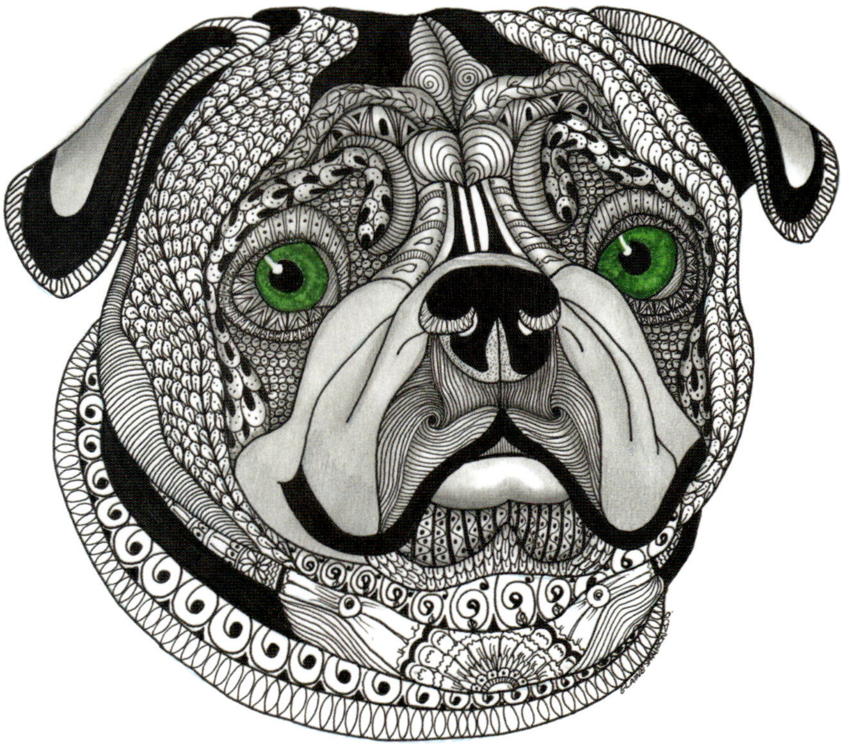

By Elaine Sampson (DO#1106)

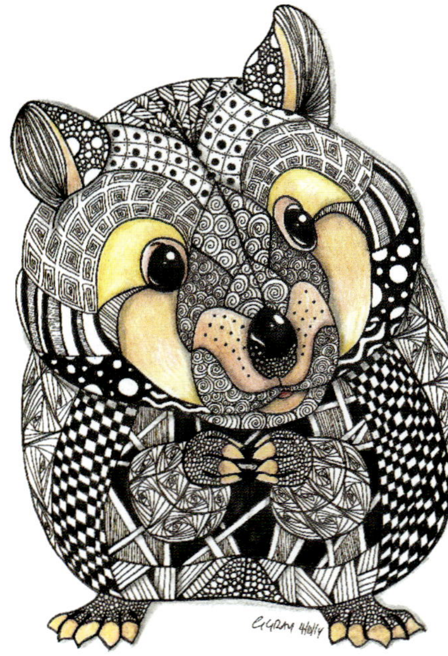

By Abbey Gray (DO#1107)

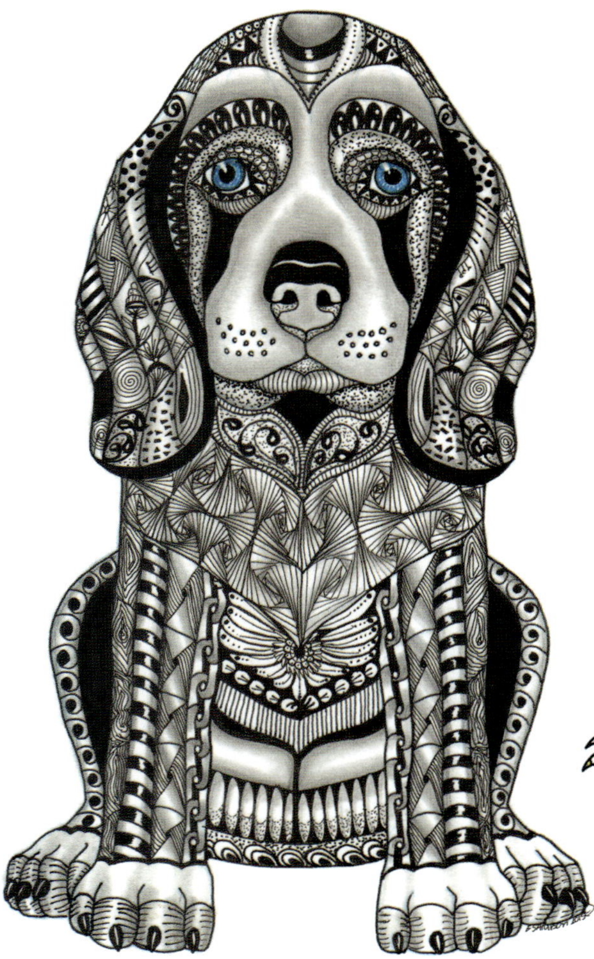

By Elaine Sampson (DO#1102)

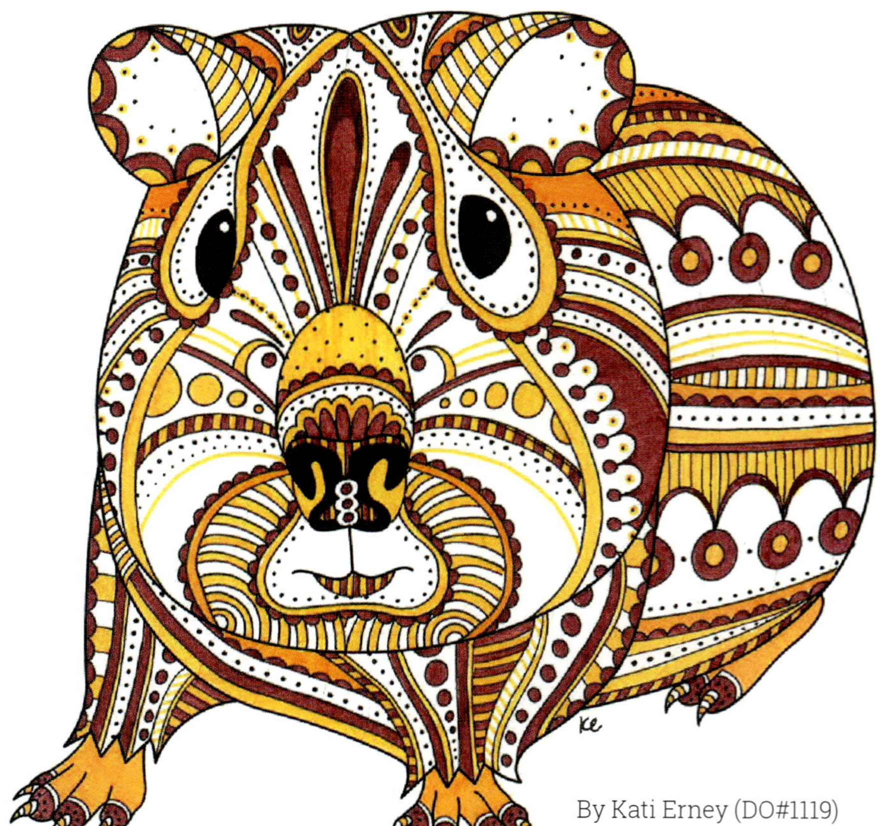

By Kati Erney (DO#1119)

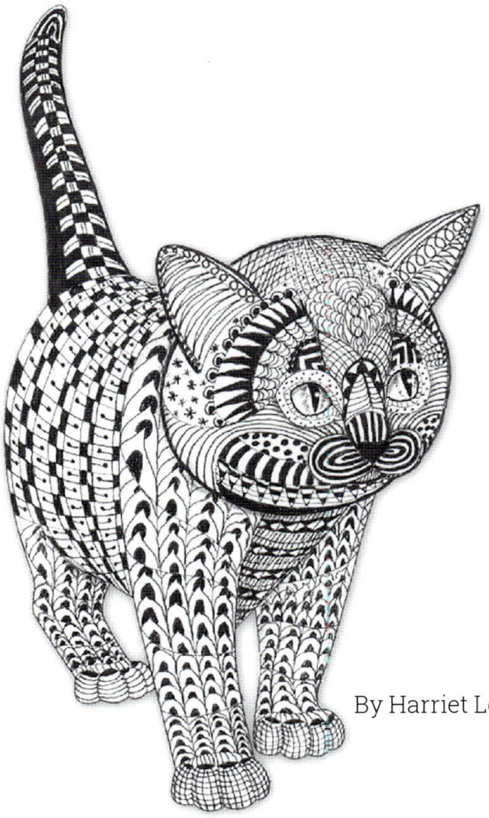

By Harriet Loftus (DO#1094)

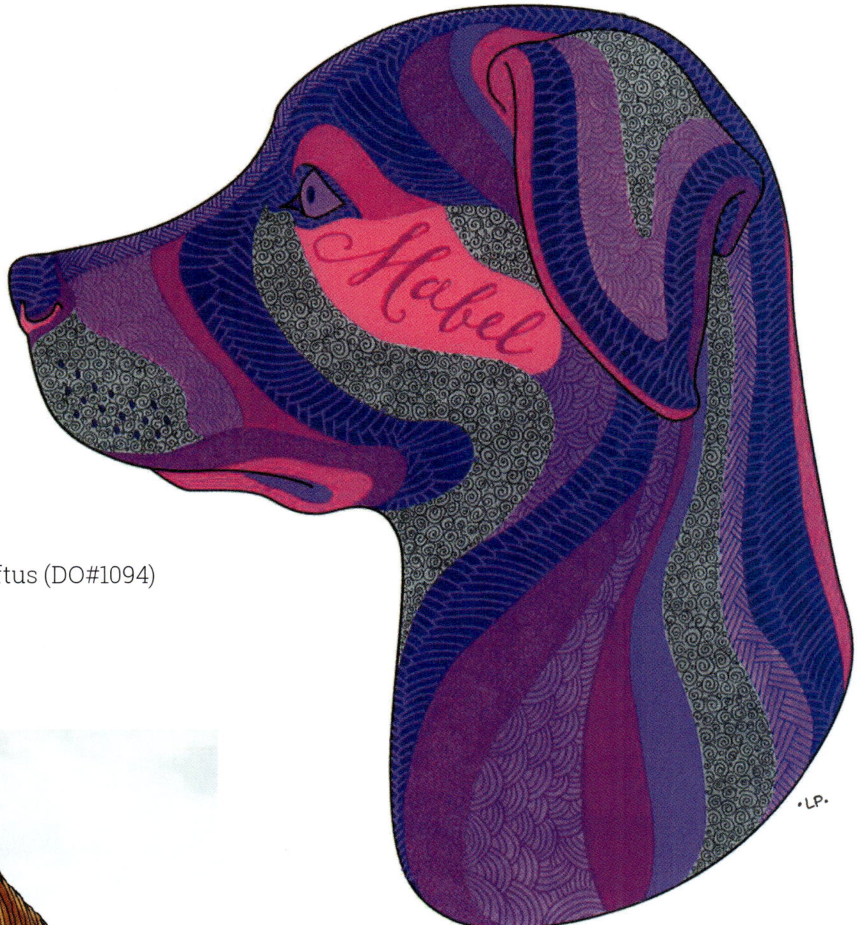

By Llara Pazdan (DO#1117)

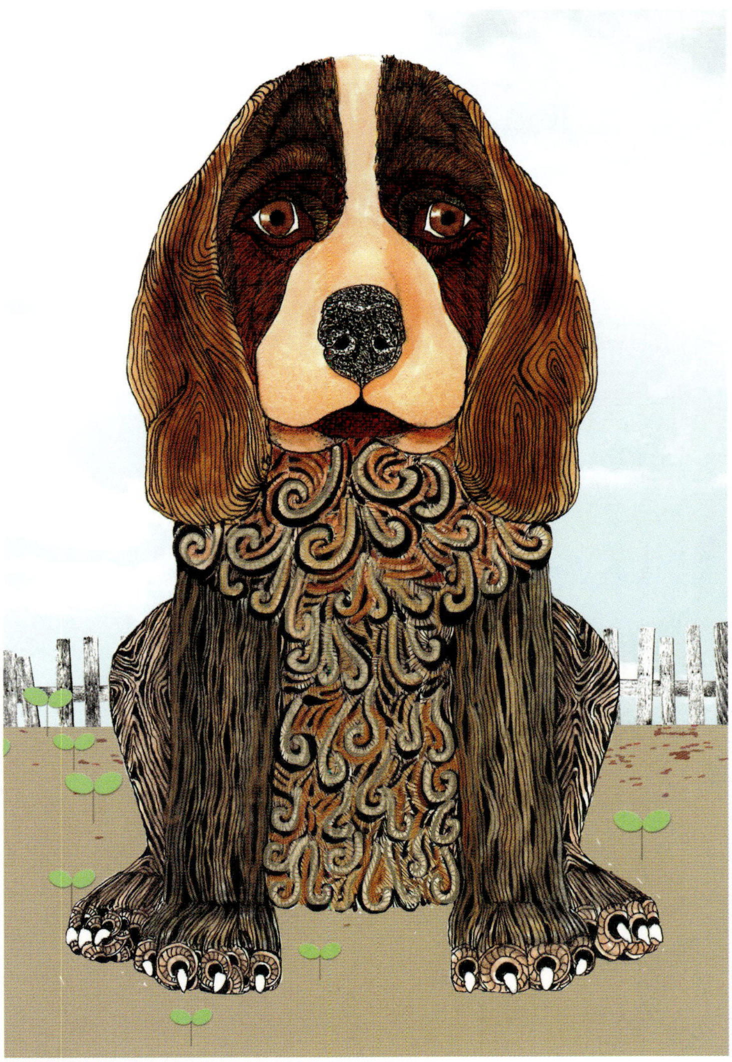

By Linda McMillen (DO#1102)

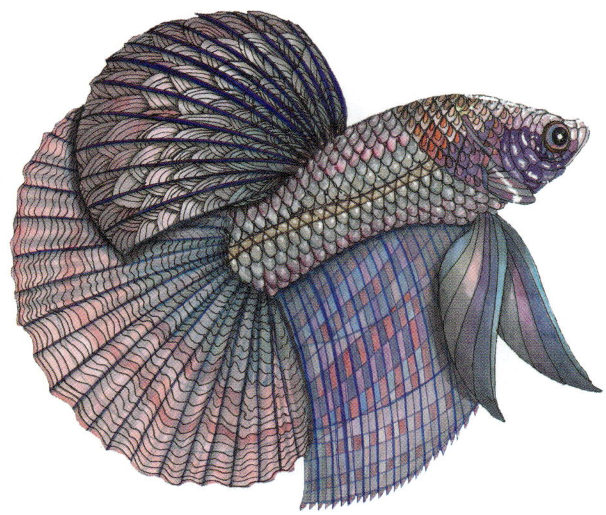

By Linda McMillen (DO#1104)

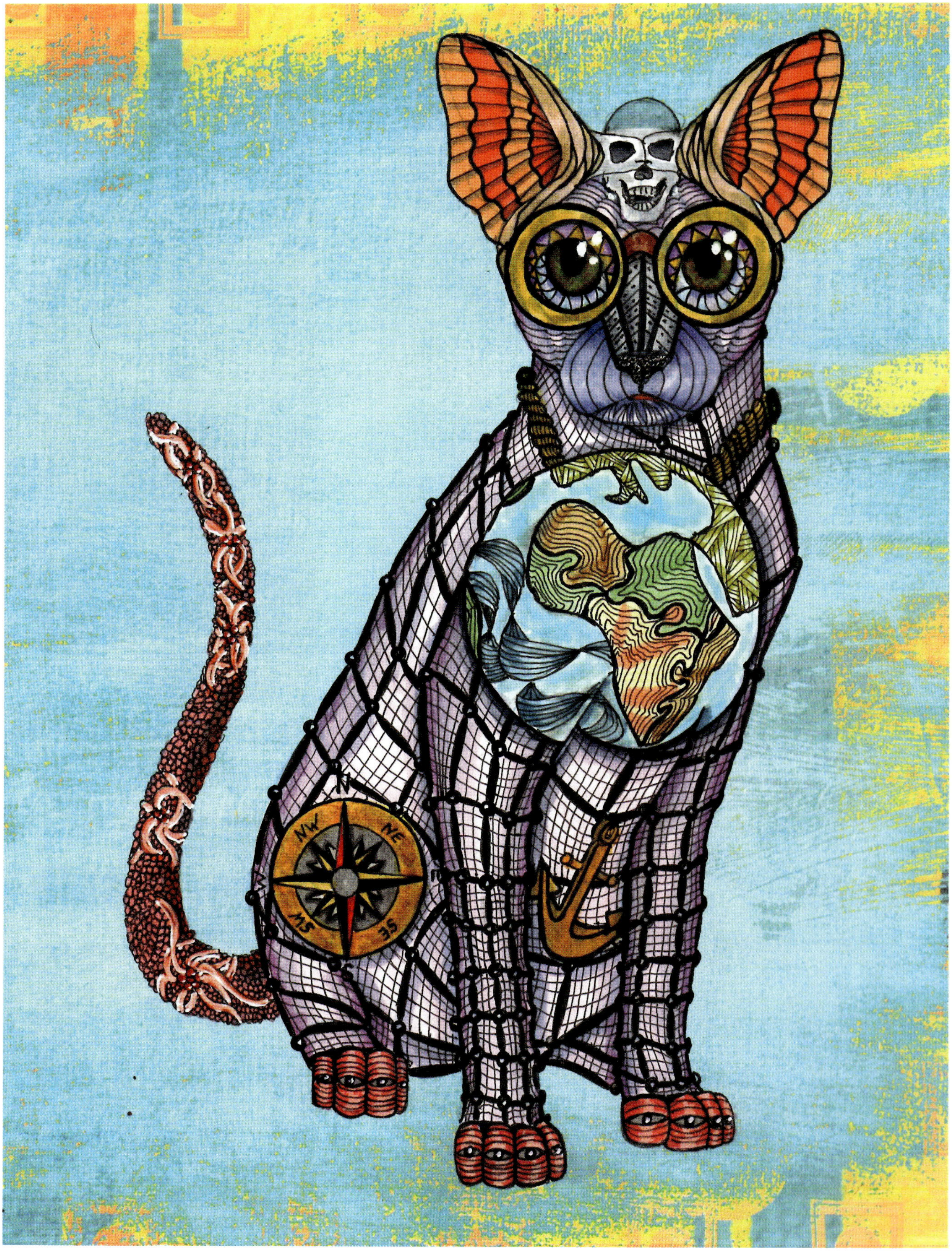

By Linda McMillen (DO#1105)

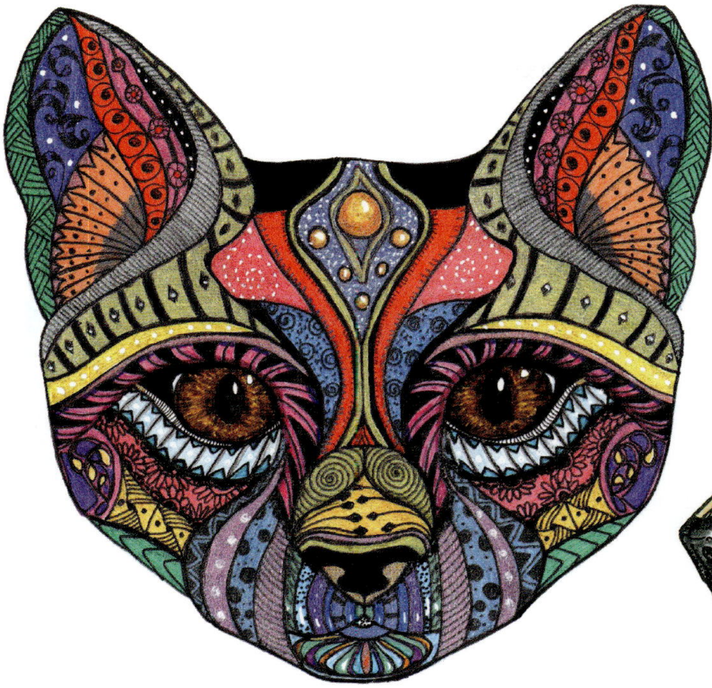

By Elaine Sampson (DO#1098)

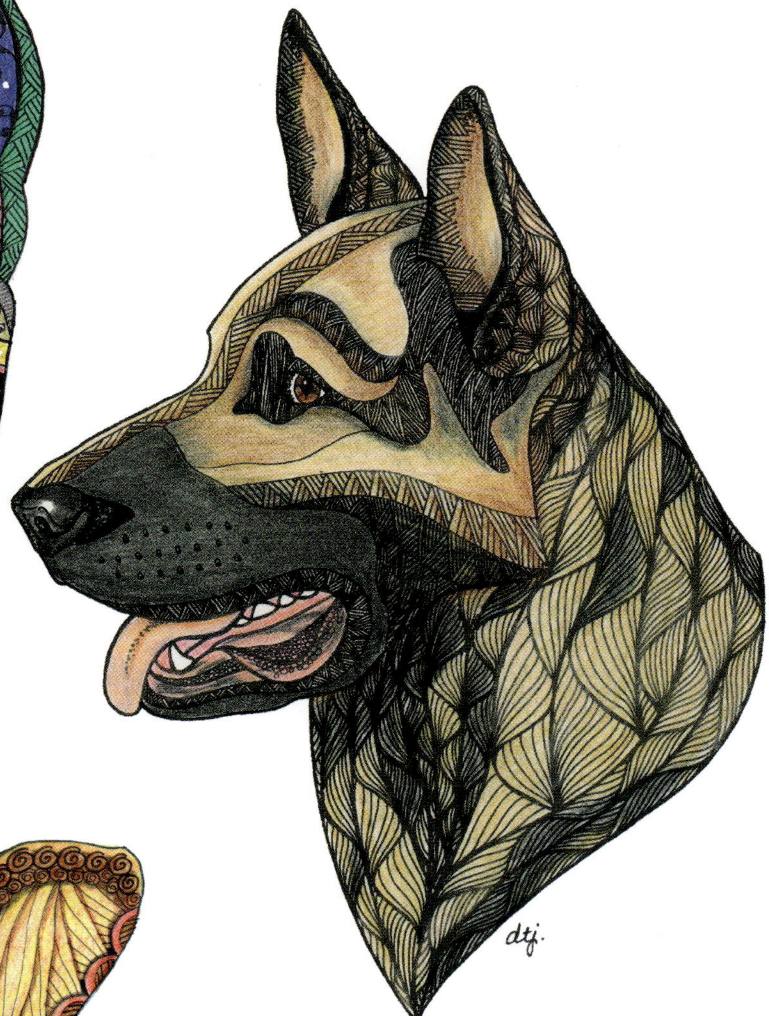

By Darla Tjelmeland (DO#1113)

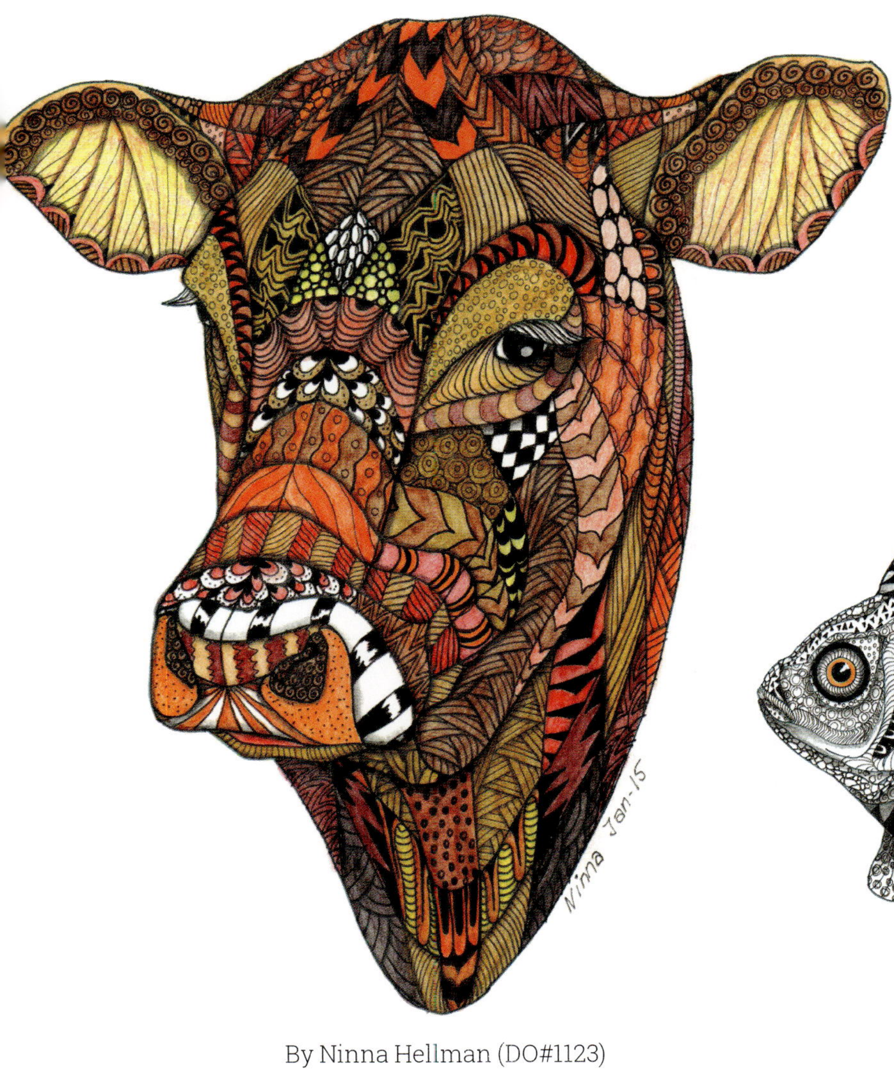

By Ninna Hellman (DO#1123)

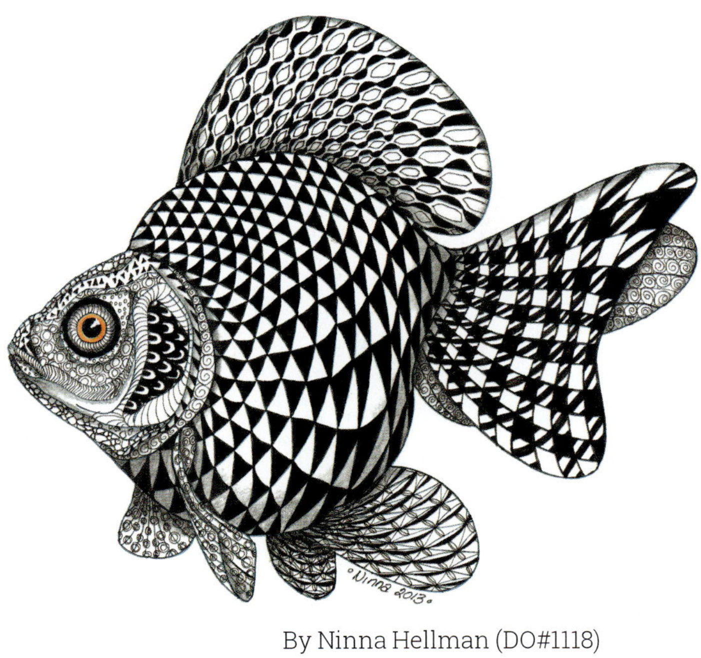

By Ninna Hellman (DO#1118)

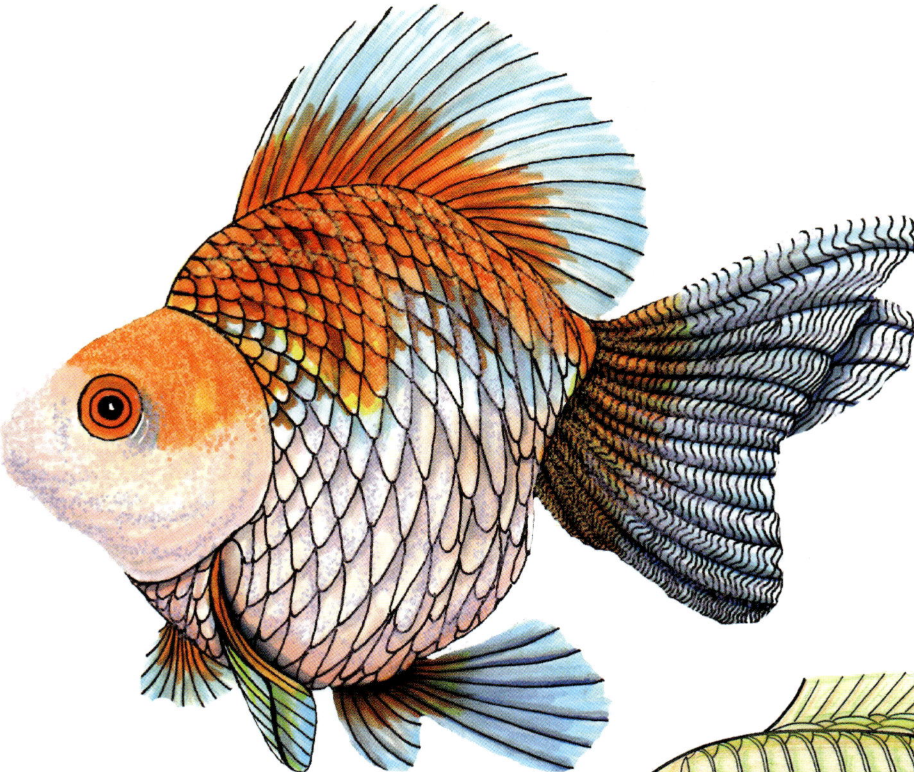

By Linda McMillen (DO#1118)

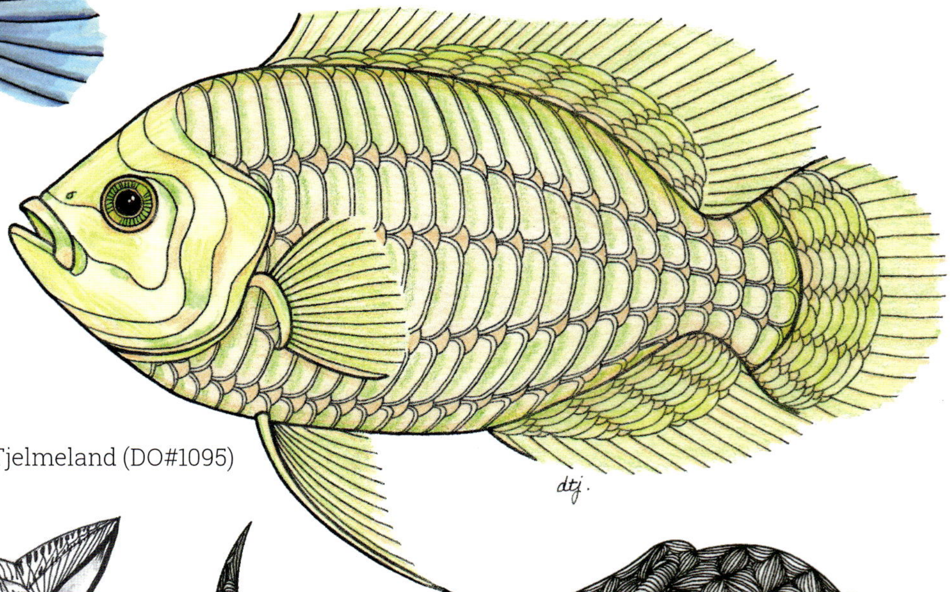

By Darla Tjelmeland (DO#1095)

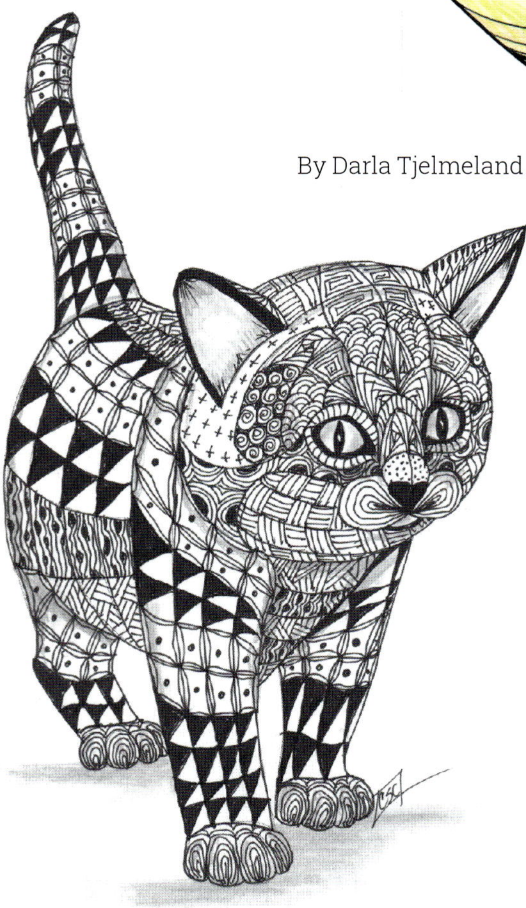

By Cathy Cusson (DO#1094)

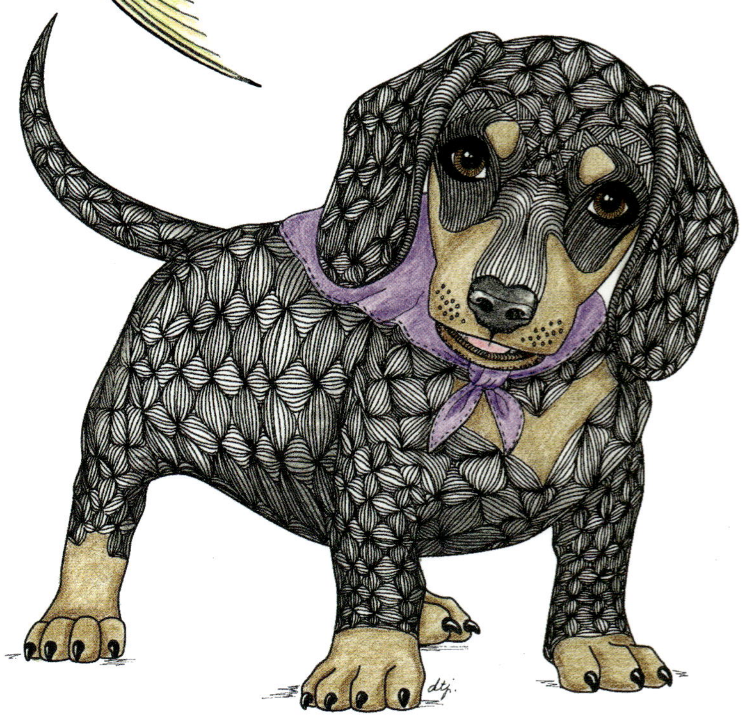

By Darla Tjelmeland (DO#1124)

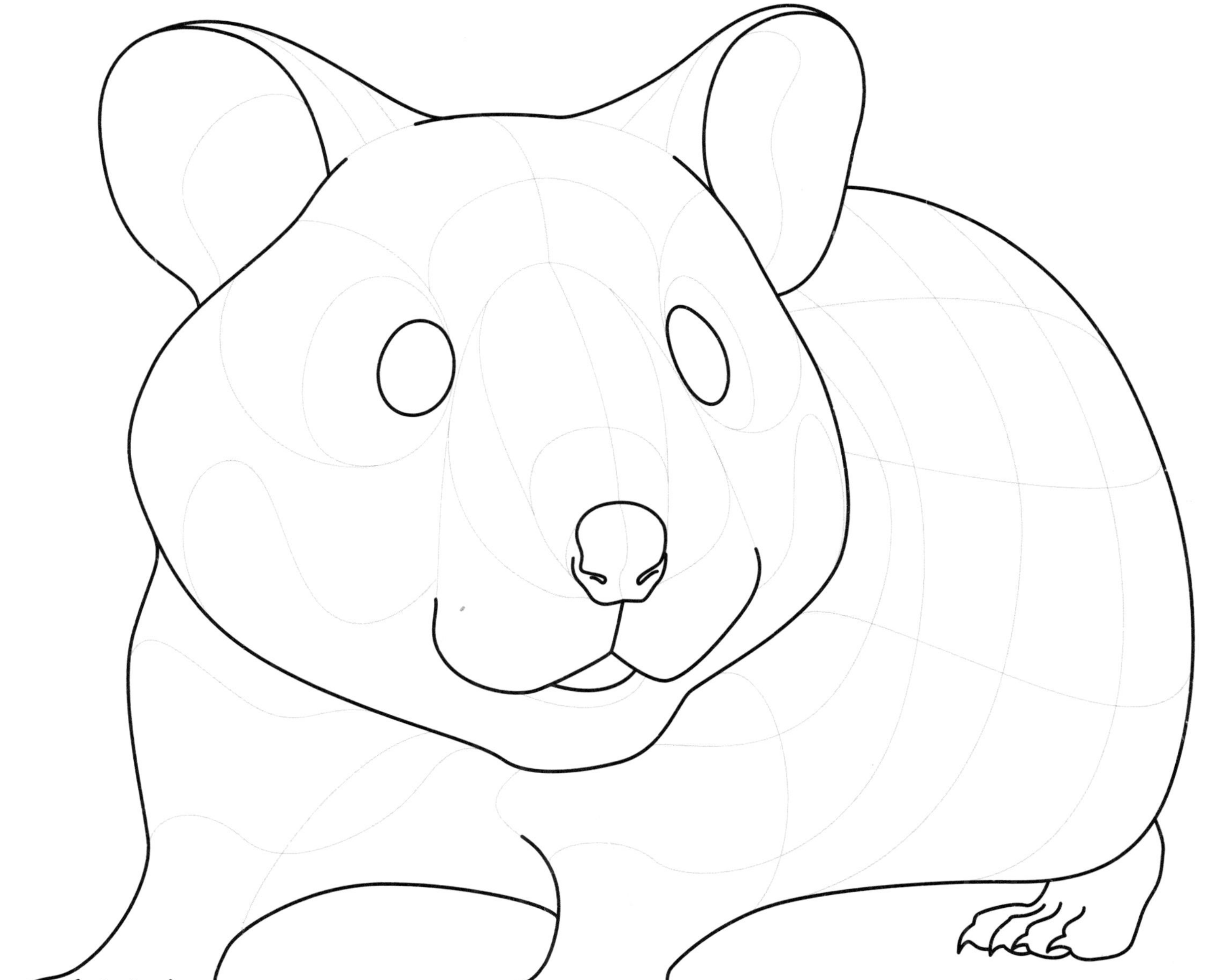

Animals are like little angels sent to earth to teach us how to love.

—Whitney Mandel

DO#1093, Hampster:

The Syrian hamster is the most common pet hamster and is also known as the teddy bear hamster or golden hamster. It usually grows to about 6 inches (15 cm) in length.

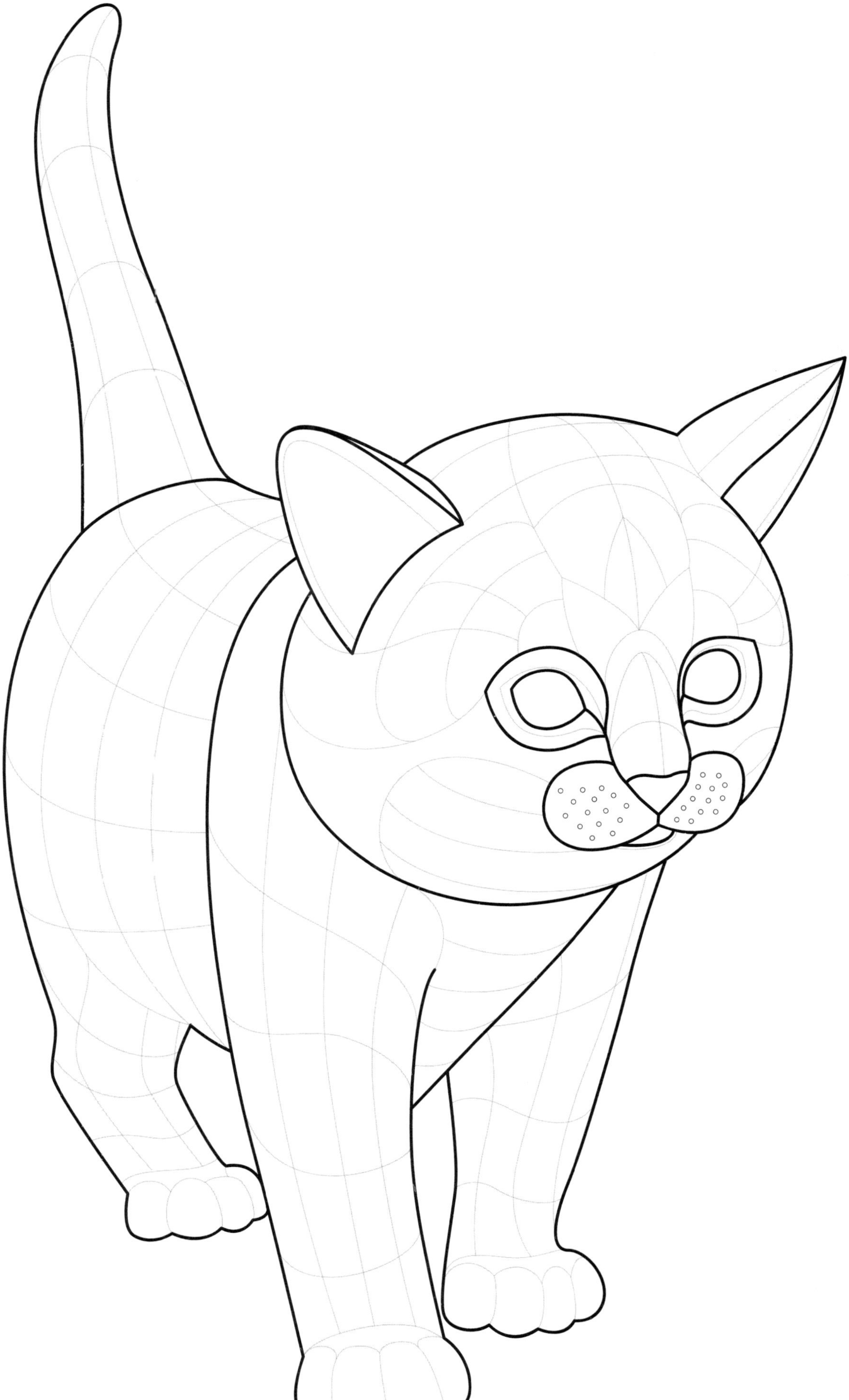

There is no more intrepid explorer than a kitten.

—Jules Champfleury

DO#1094, Kitten:

The nose pad of a cat is ridged in a unique pattern, just as a fingerprint is unique to each person.

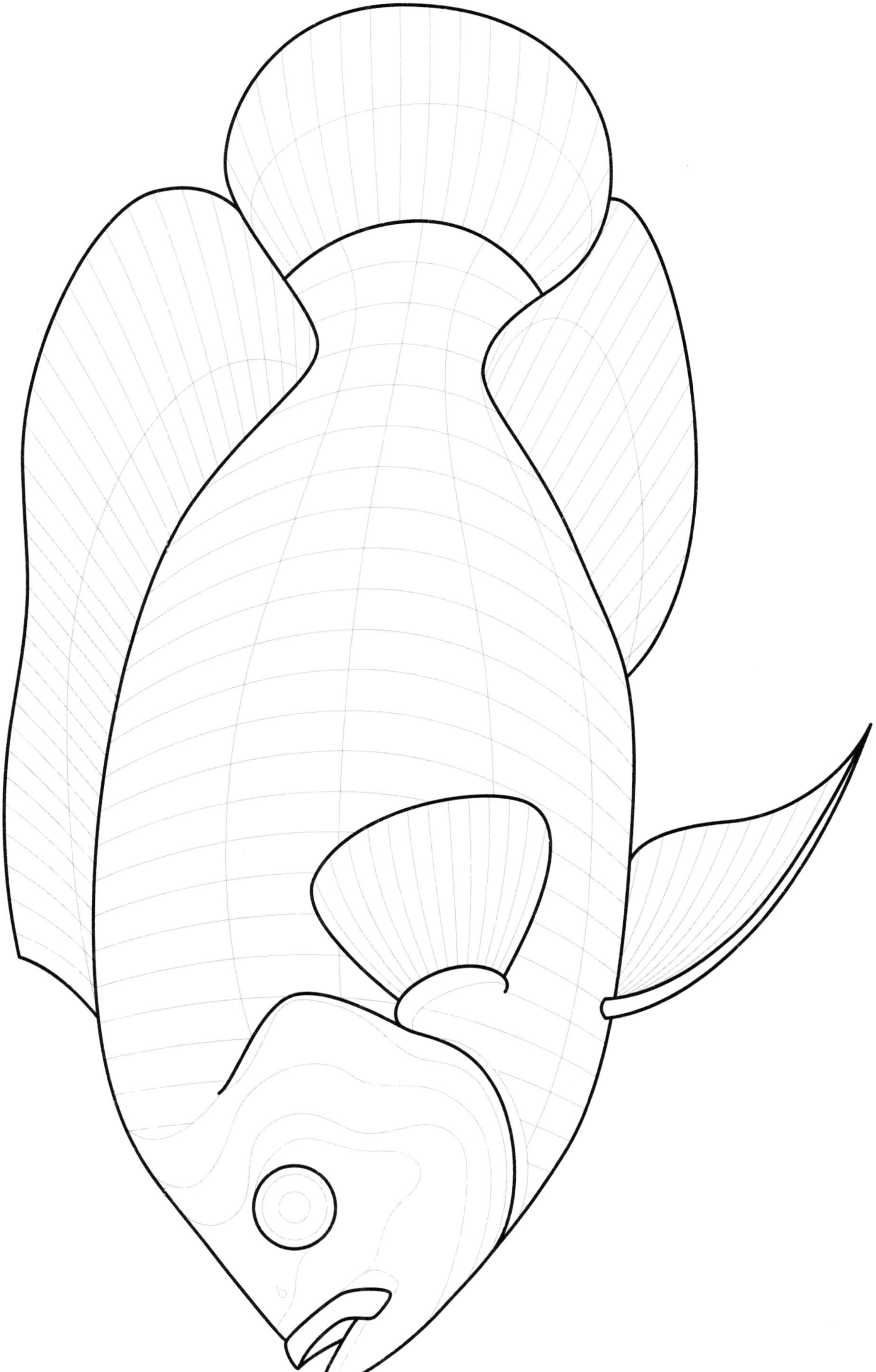

A friend is what the heart needs all the time.

—Henry Van Dyke

DO#1095, Oscar Fish:

Oscar fish love attention and enjoy playing—
many people give their Oscar a ping-pong ball to play with in the tank!

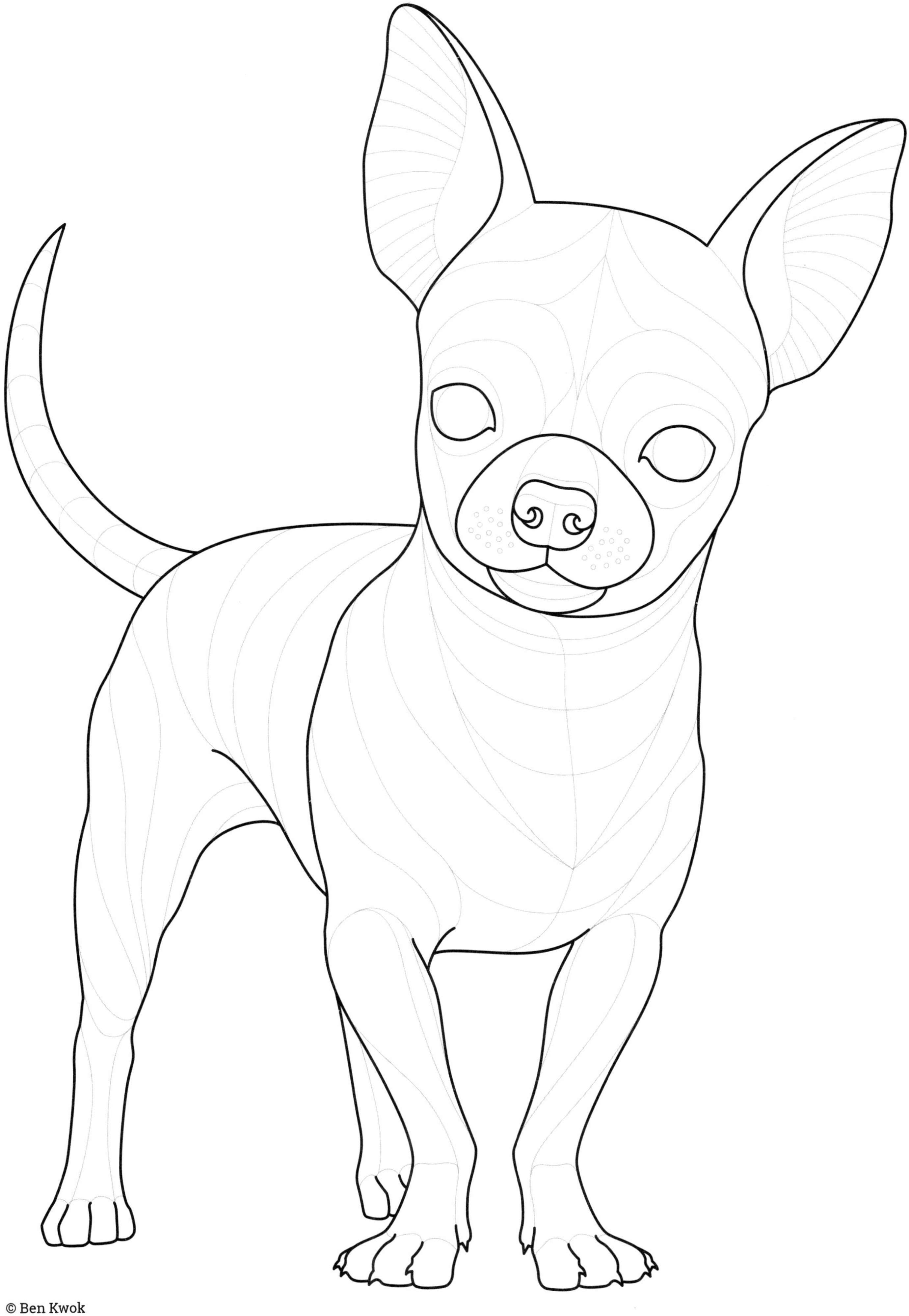

Our pets are our family.

—Unknown

DG#1096, Chihuahua:

The Chihuahua is the smallest breed of dog in the world, measuring up to 9 inches (23 cm) tall and weighing only 4 to 7 pounds (2-3 kg).

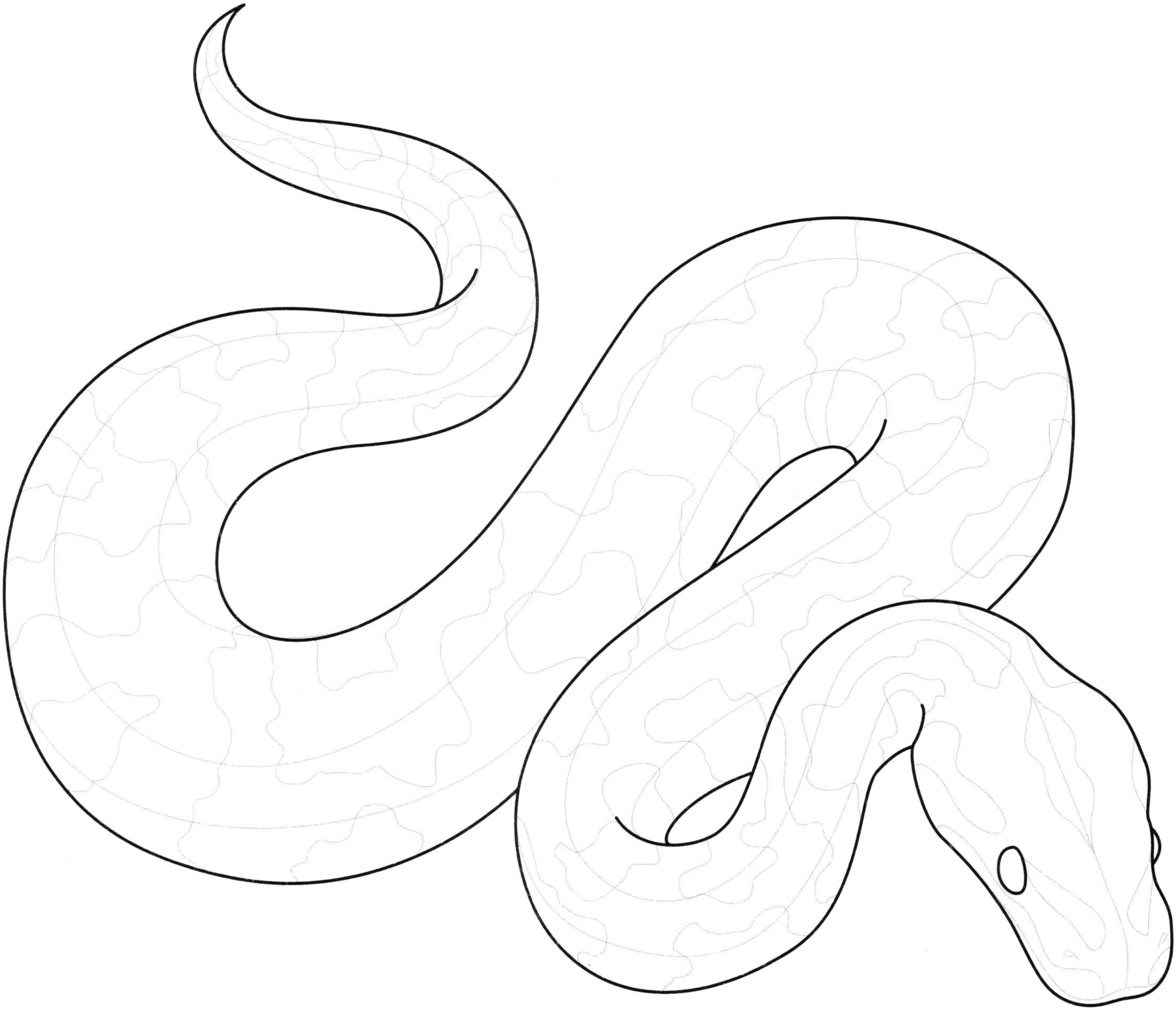

Perhaps the greatest gift an animal
has to offer is a permanent reminder
of who we really are.

—Nick Trout

DO#1097, Ball Python:
When a ball python is threatened in the wild, it will roll up into a ball with its head protected in the center of the coil.

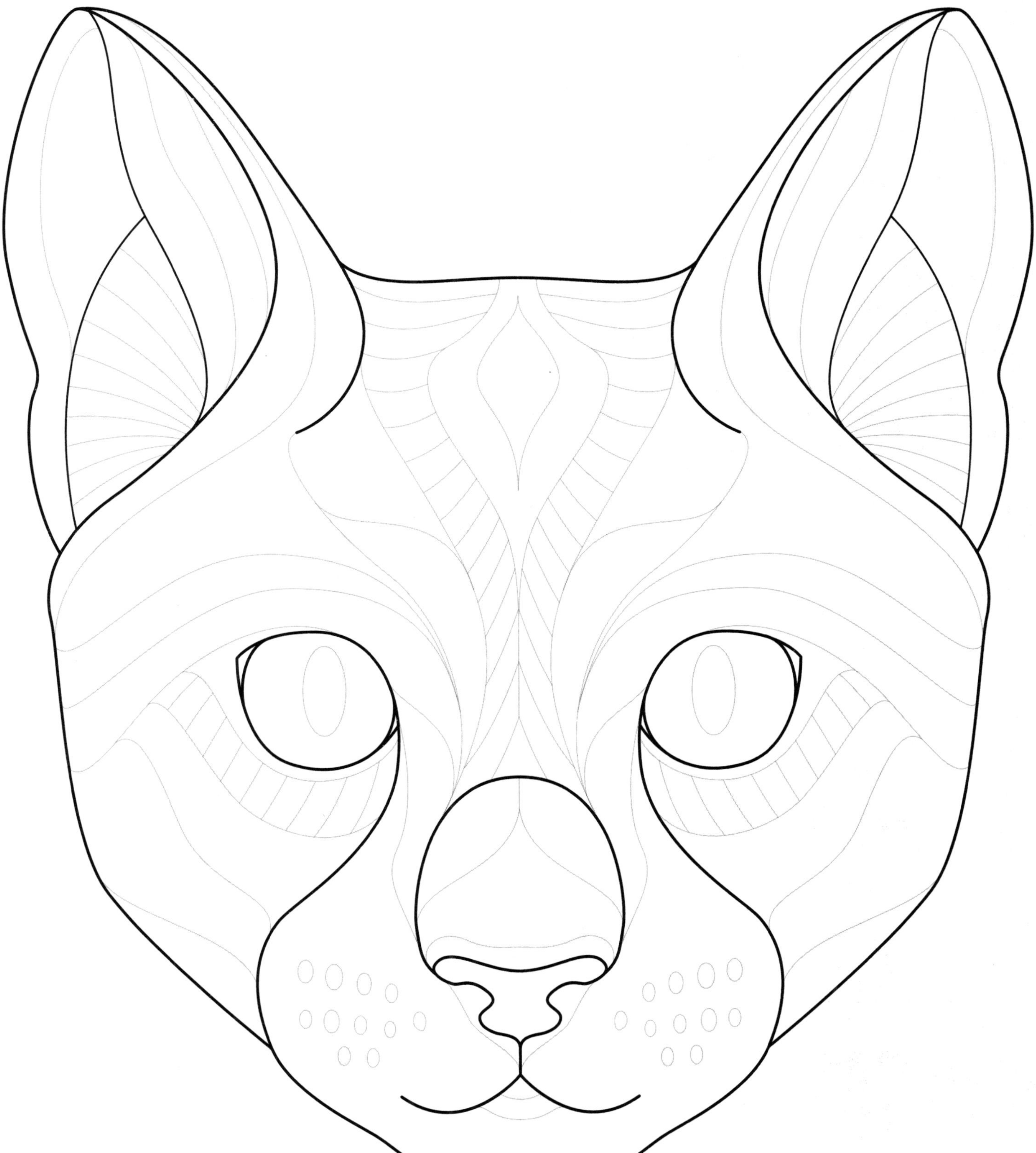

In ancient times cats were worshipped as gods;
they have not forgotten this.

—Terry Pratchett

DO#1098, Cat:

A group of cats is called a clowder, a male cat is a tom, and a female cat is called a molly or queen.

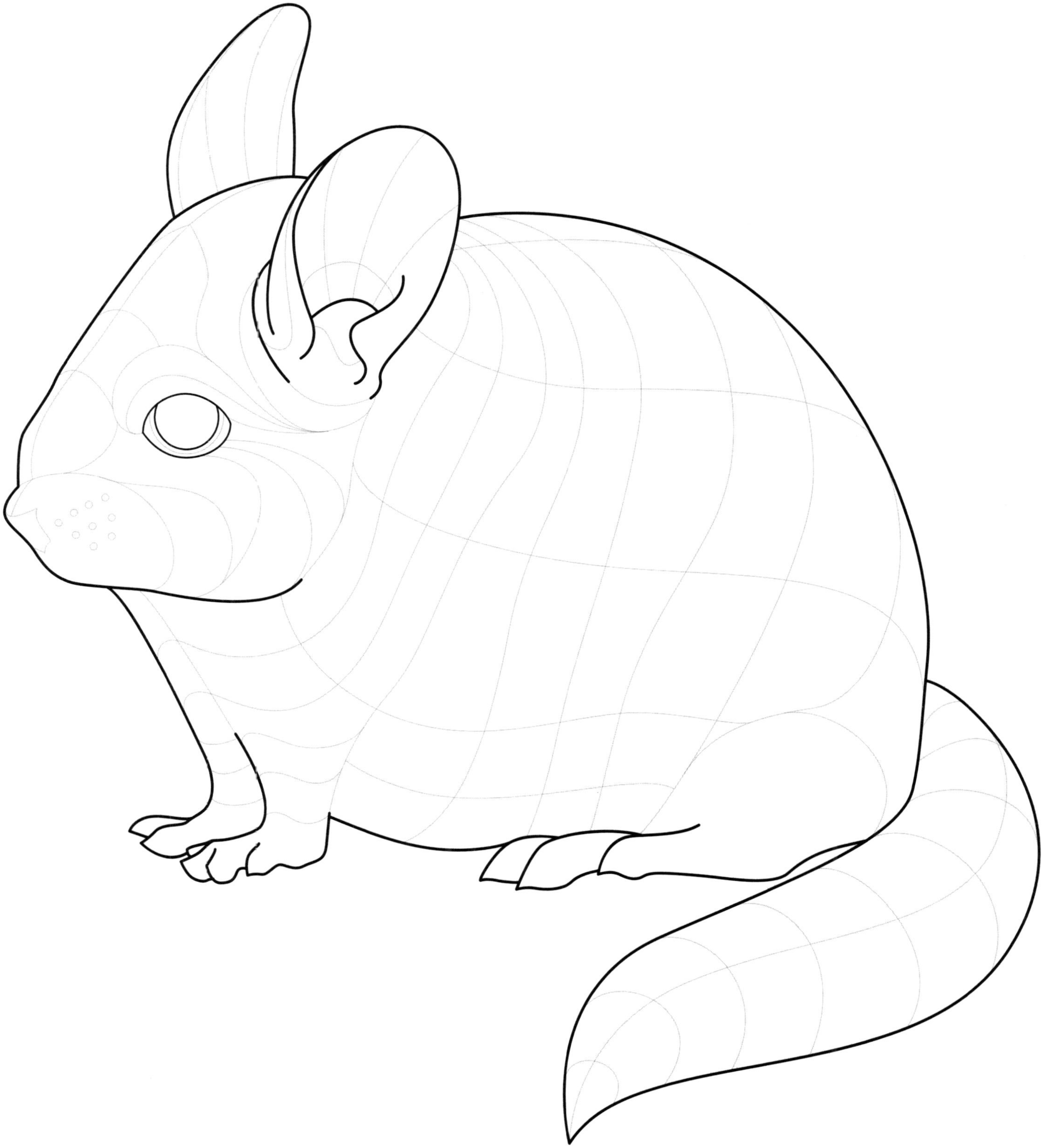

Our perfect companions never have fewer than four feet.

—Sidonie Gabrielle Colette

DO#1099, Chinchilla:

Native to the Andes Mountains of northern Chile, chinchillas have luxuriously soft fur and are very active.

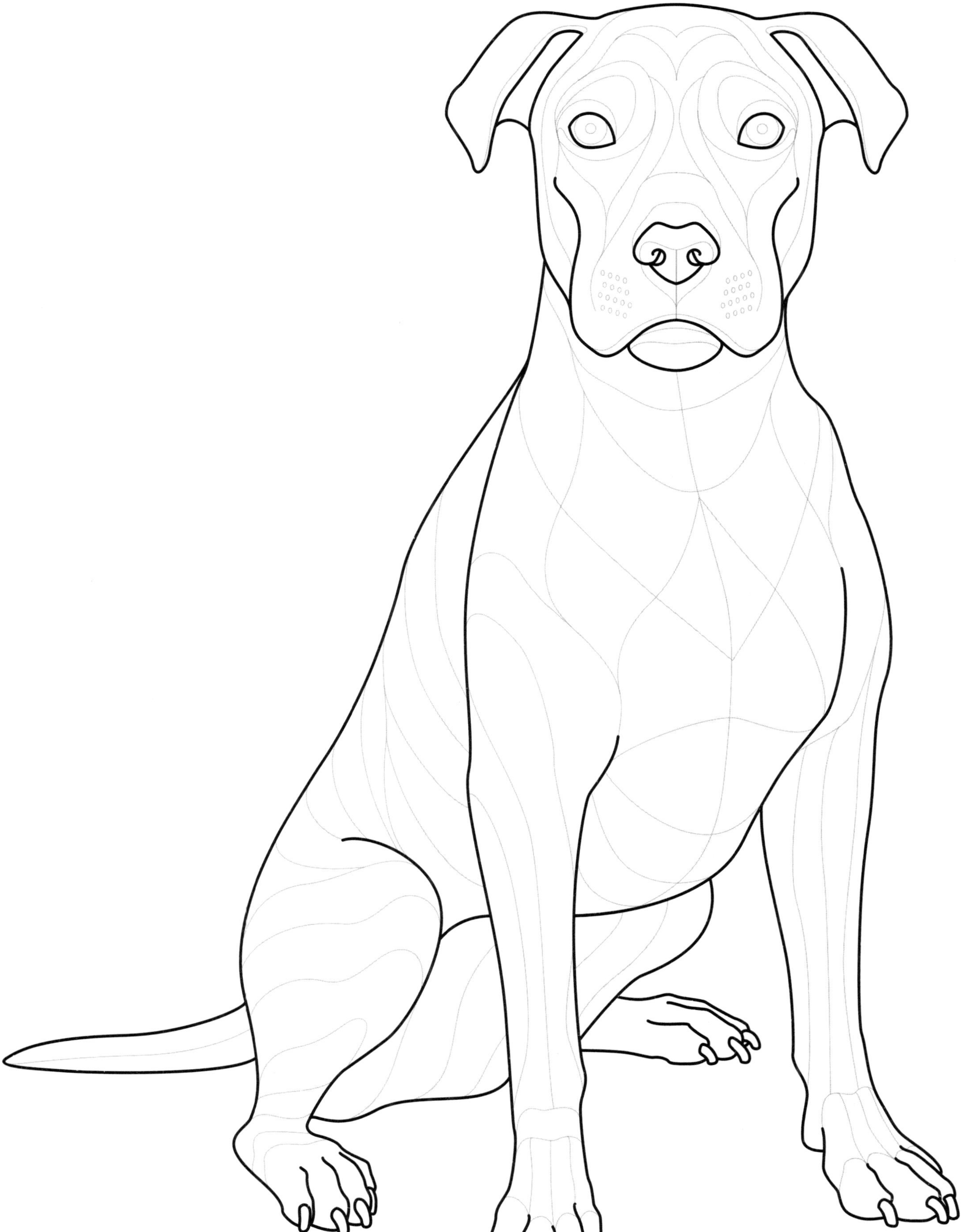

Dogs are not our whole life, but they make our lives whole.

—Roger Caras

DO#1100, Pit Bull:

Pit bull puppies often have wrinkled foreheads; as they grow, the skin stretches and becomes smooth.

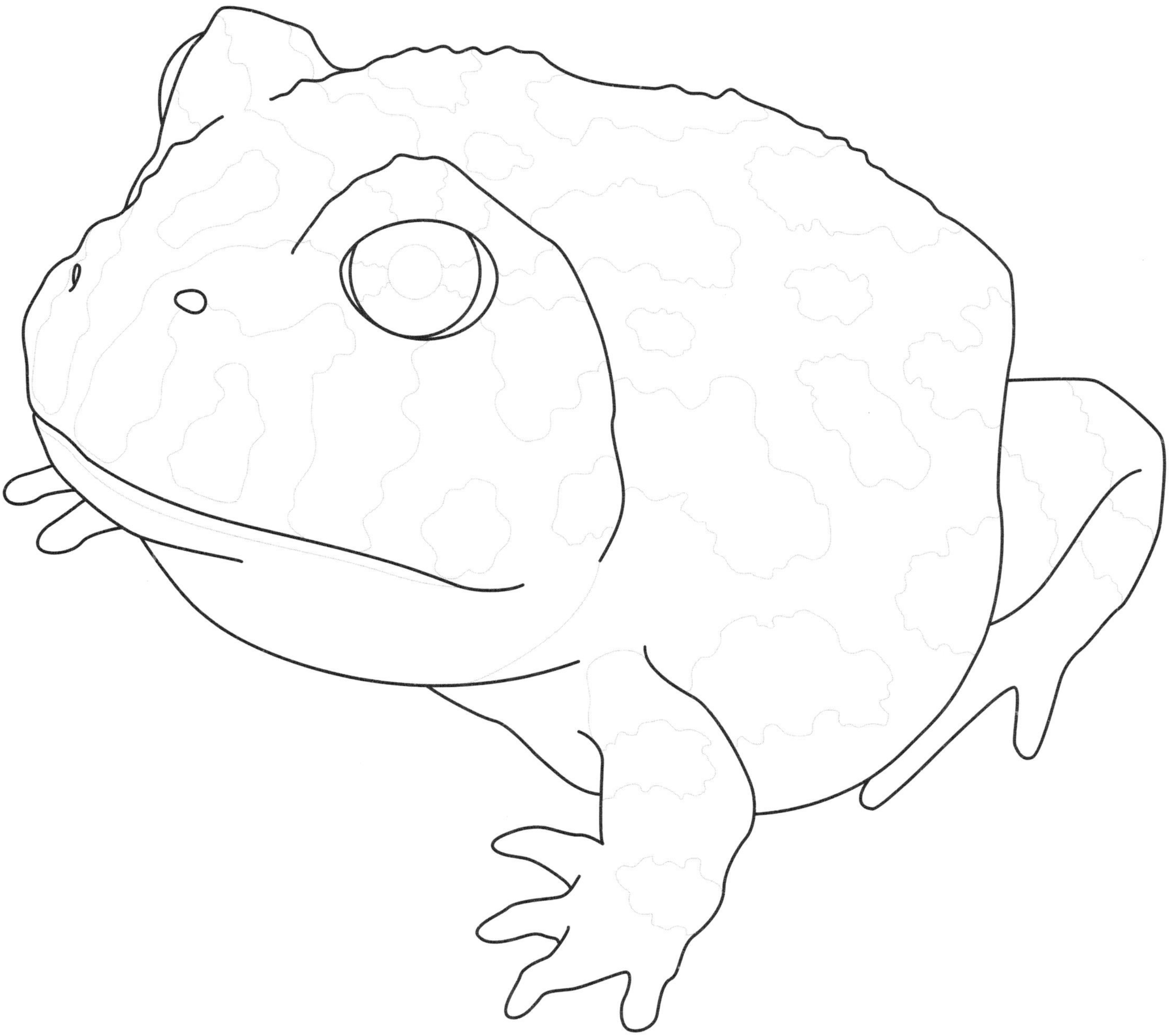

I think having an animal in your life makes you a better human.

—Unknown

DO#1101, Pacman Frog:

With their round shape and large mouth, these cute frogs really do resemble the classic video game character!

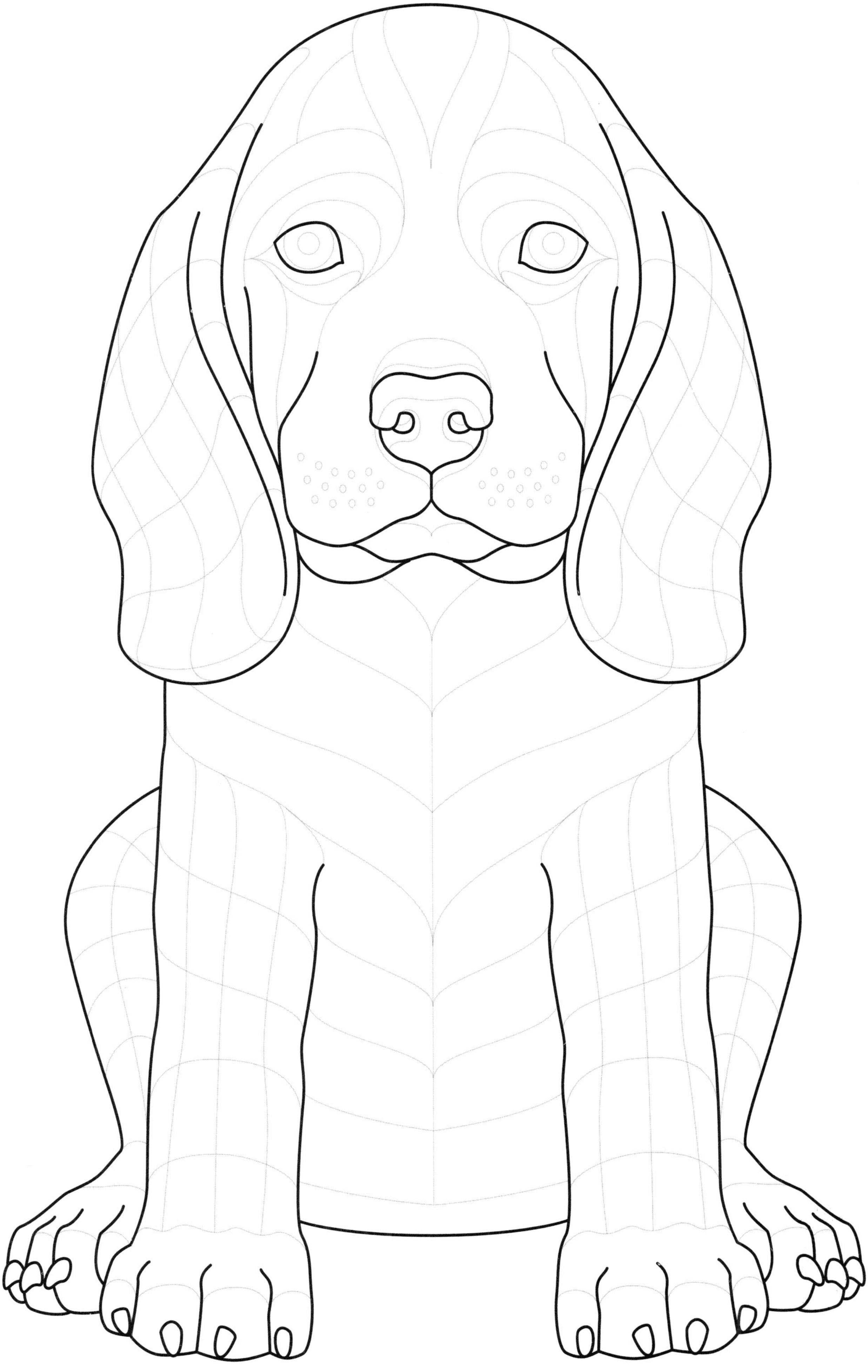

Happiness is a warm puppy.

—Charles M. Schulz

DO#1102, Beagle:

A vocal, intelligent, active dog, beagles have an amazing sense of smell and excel as police dogs sniffing out contraband at airports.

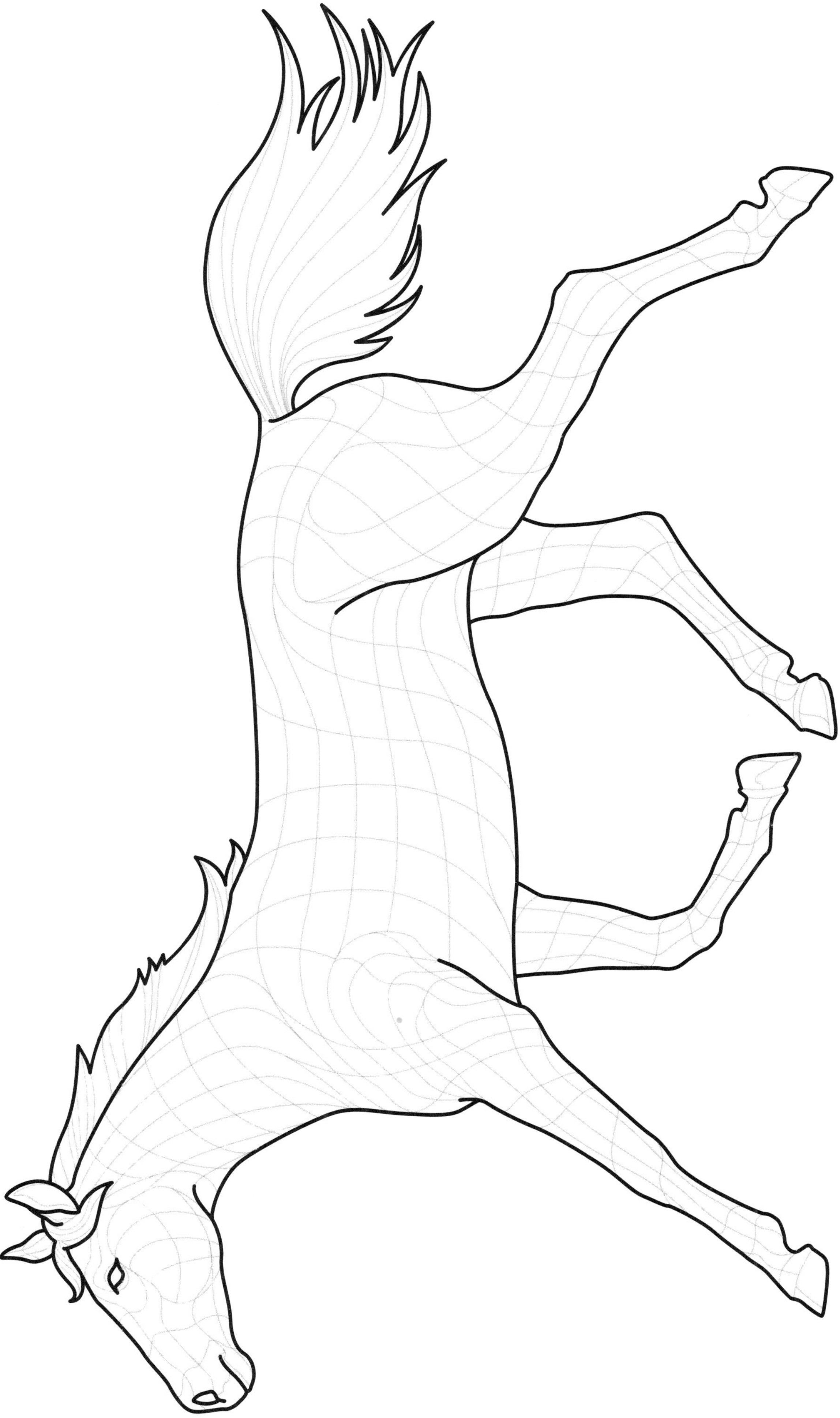

A horse gallops with his lungs,
Perseveres with his heart,
And wins with his character.

—Federico Tesio

DO#1103, Horse:

Domesticated around 4,000 years ago, the horse has been an important and beloved part of human society.

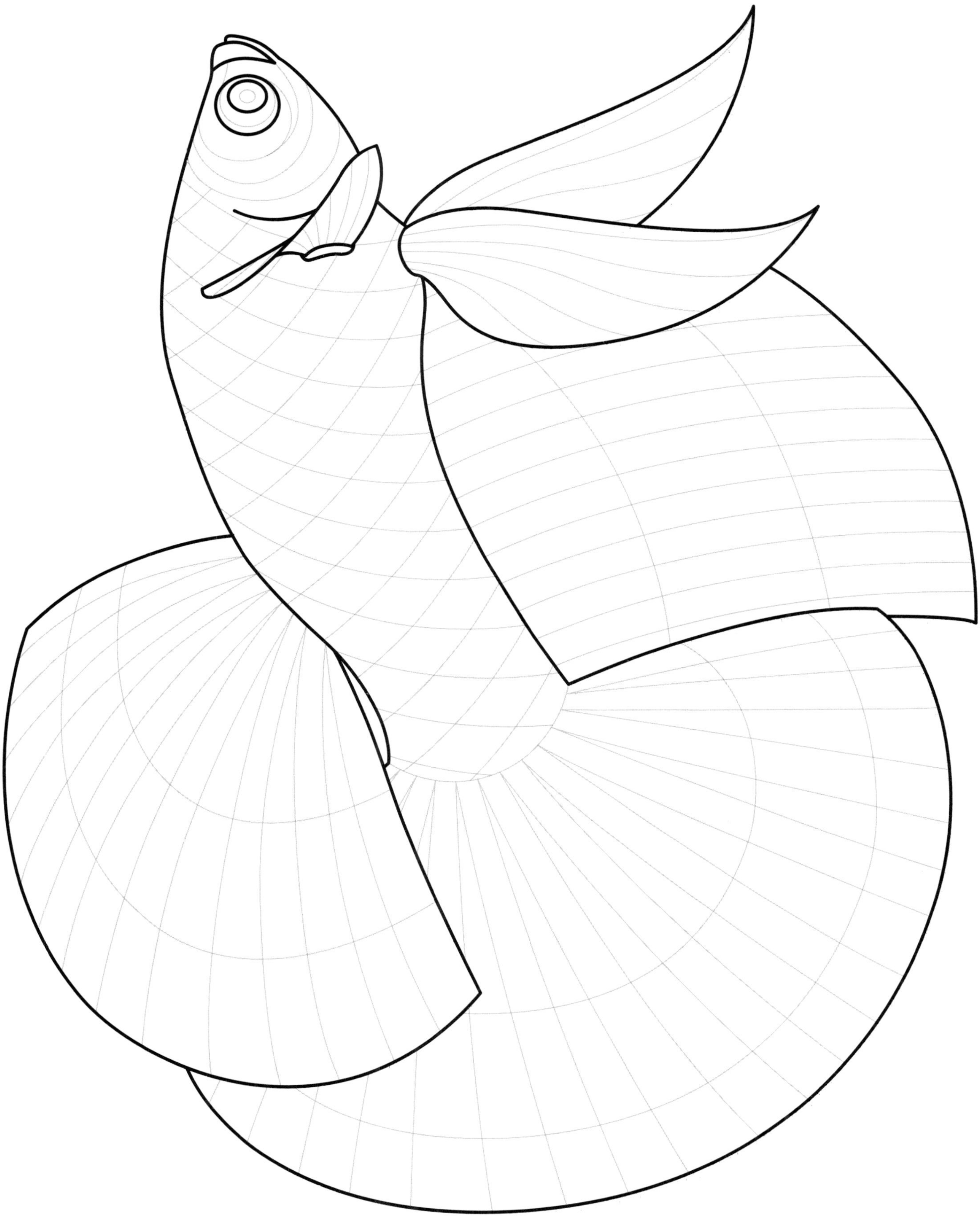

They show us what's missing in our lives,
and how to love ourselves more
completely and unconditionally.

—Trisha McCagh

DO#1104, Betta Fish:

Betta fish — previously known as Siamese fighting fish — are native to the rice paddies of Thailand, Indonesia, Malaysia, Vietnam, and parts of China.

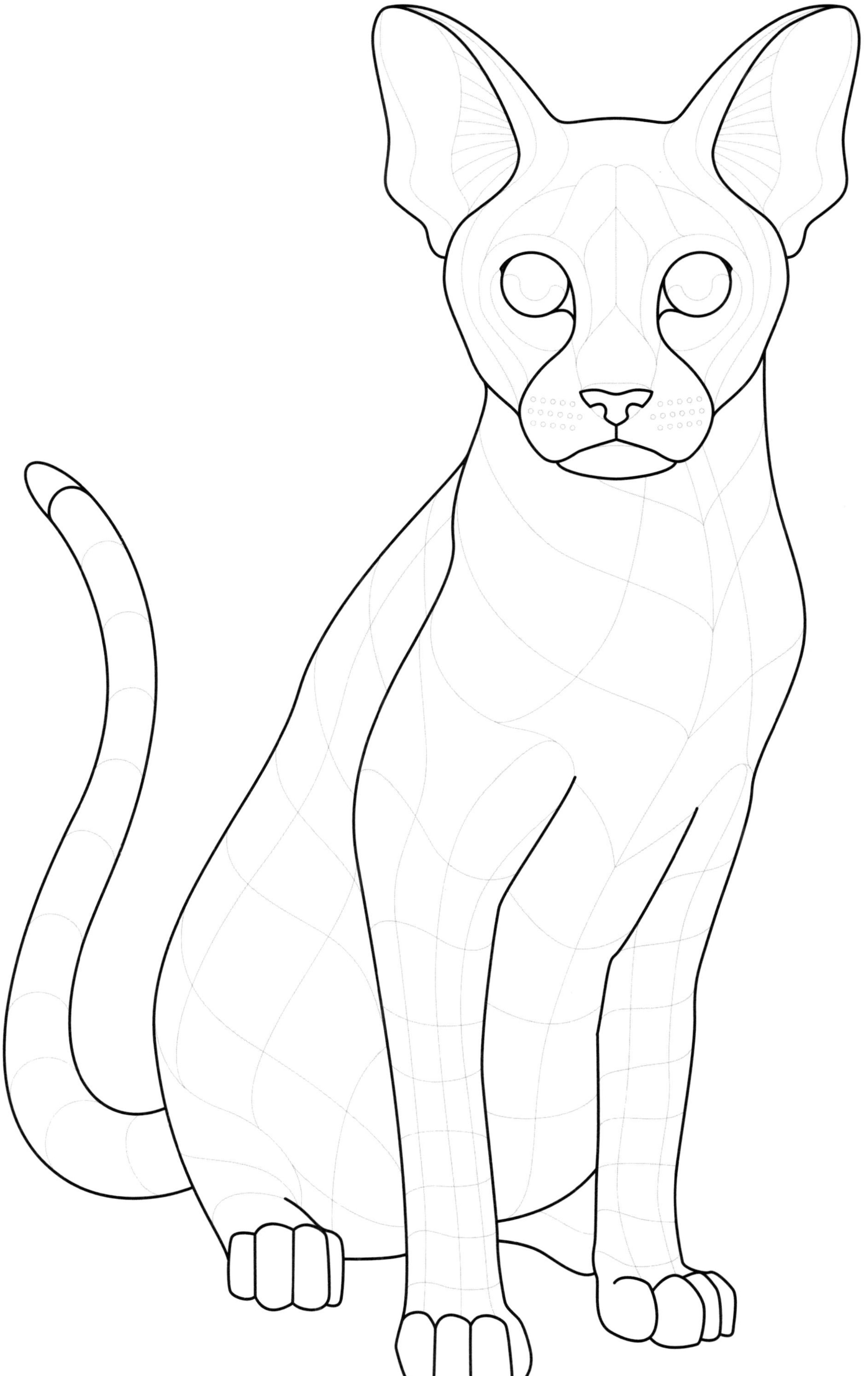

He could tell by the way animals walked
that they were keeping time to some kind of music.
Maybe it was the song
in their own hearts that they walked to.

—Laura Adams Armer

DO#1105, Siamese Cat:

In Thai, their name means "moon diamond."

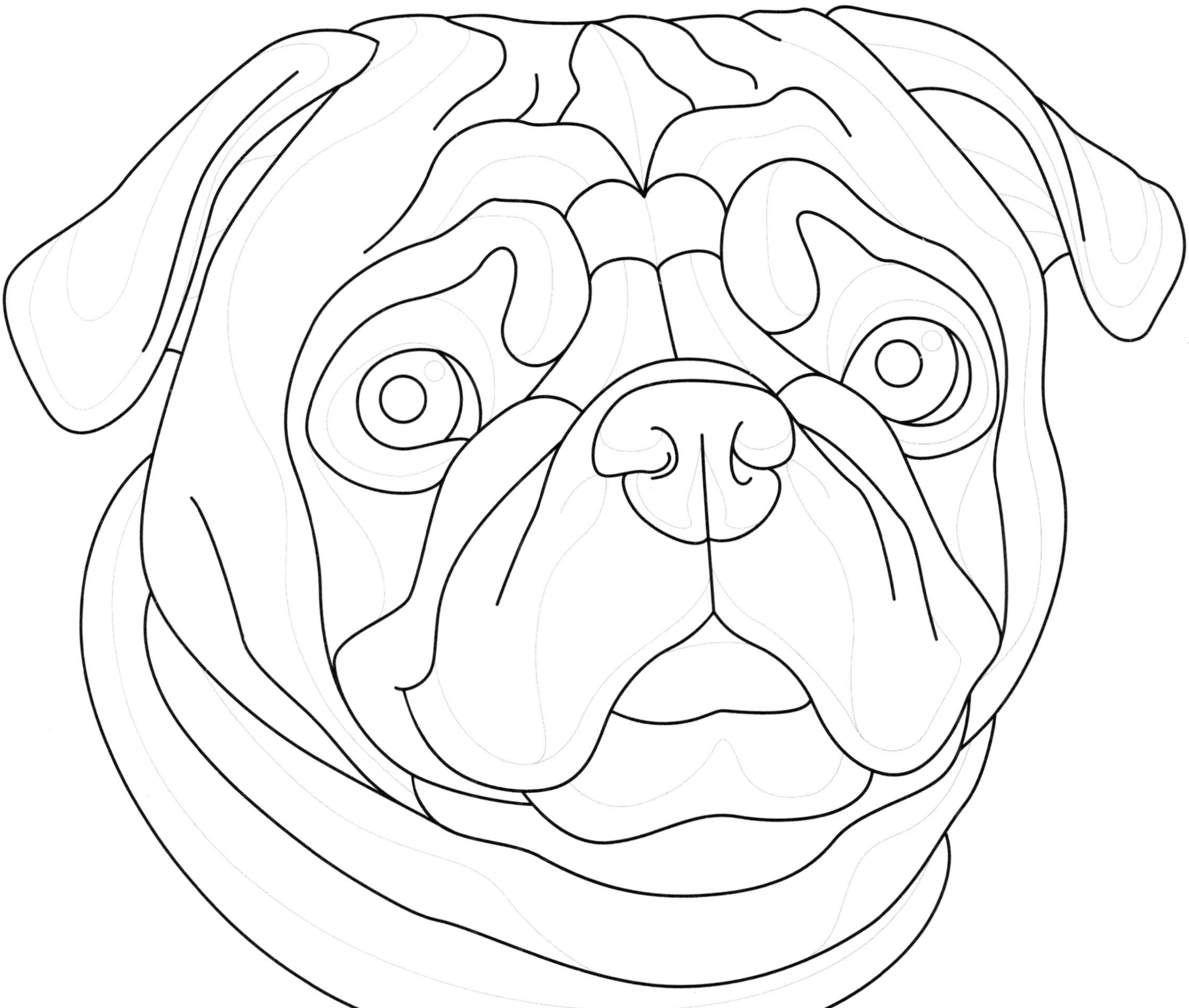

He who finds a faithful friend finds a treasure.

—Sirach

DO#1106, Pug:

Classed in the toy group of the American Kennel Club, pugs are the largest "toy" dog in the category.

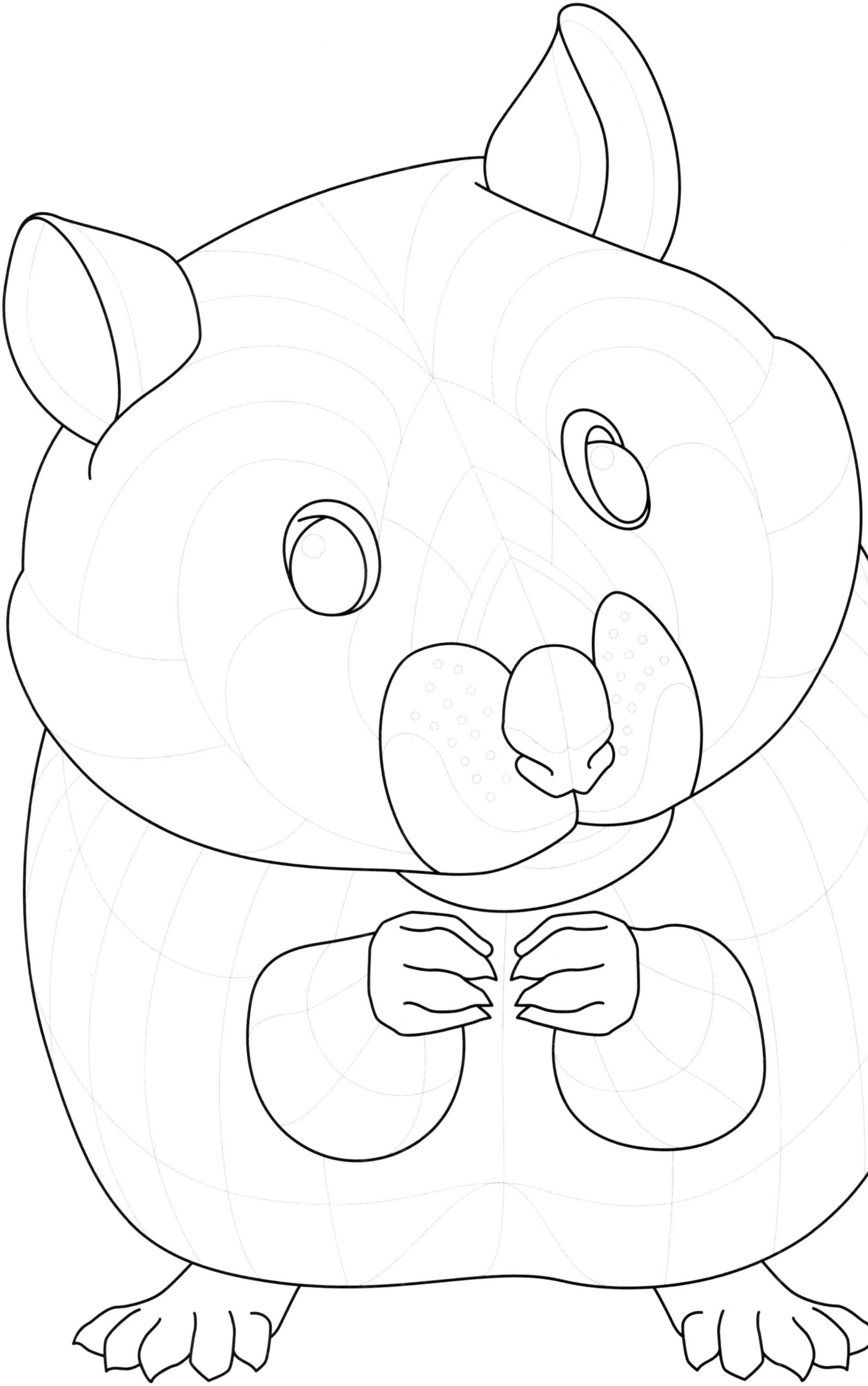

Sometimes the smallest things
take up the most room in your heart.

—Winnie the Pooh

DO#1107, Hamster:

Hamsters have very poor eyesight. With scent glands on their backs, they rub their backs against objects to leave a trail of scent to find their way around.

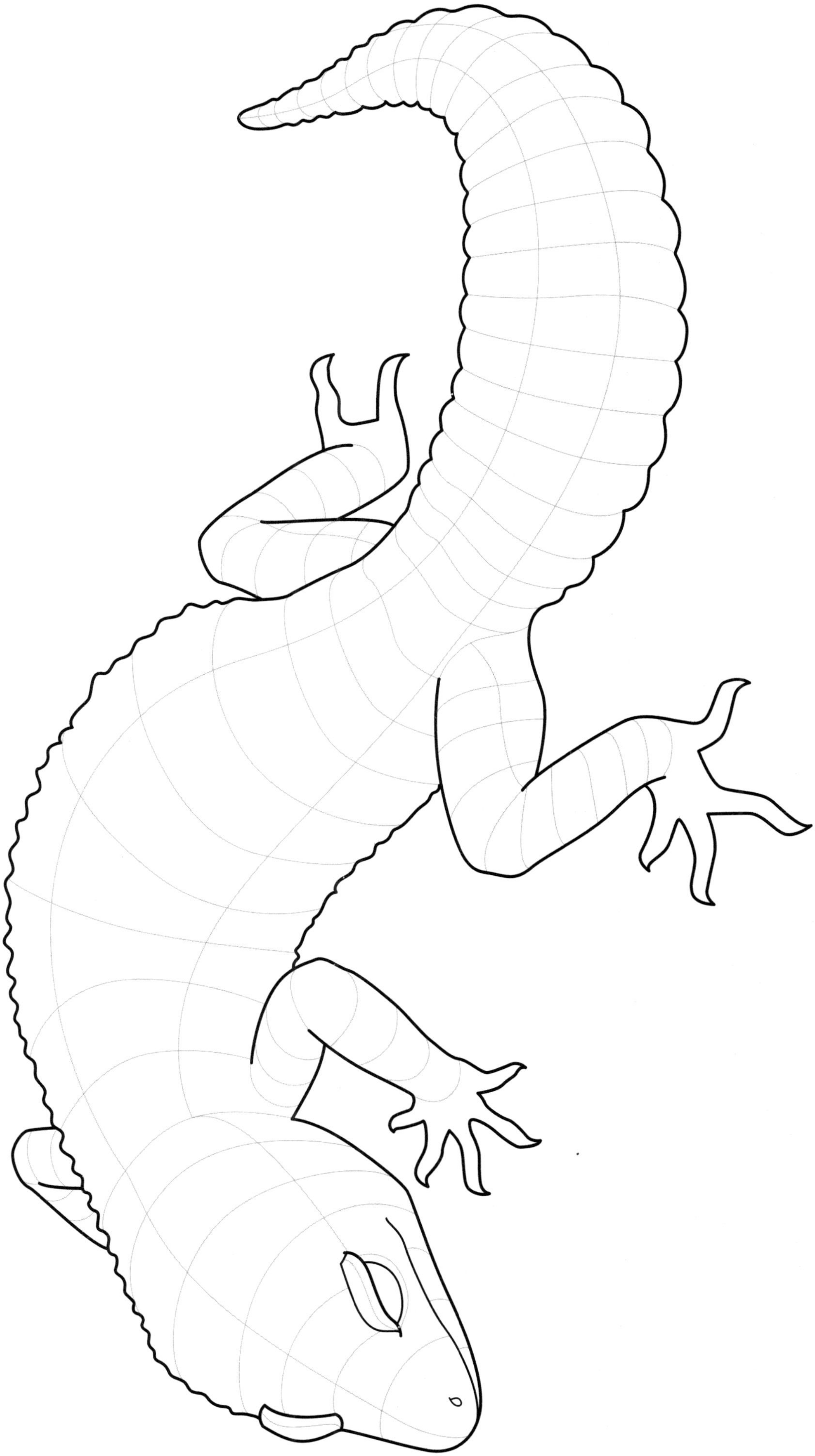

The love for all living creatures
is the most noble attribute of man.

—Charles Darwin

DO#1108, Leopard Gecko:

Leopard geckos are a very popular pet
due to their unusually gentle disposition.

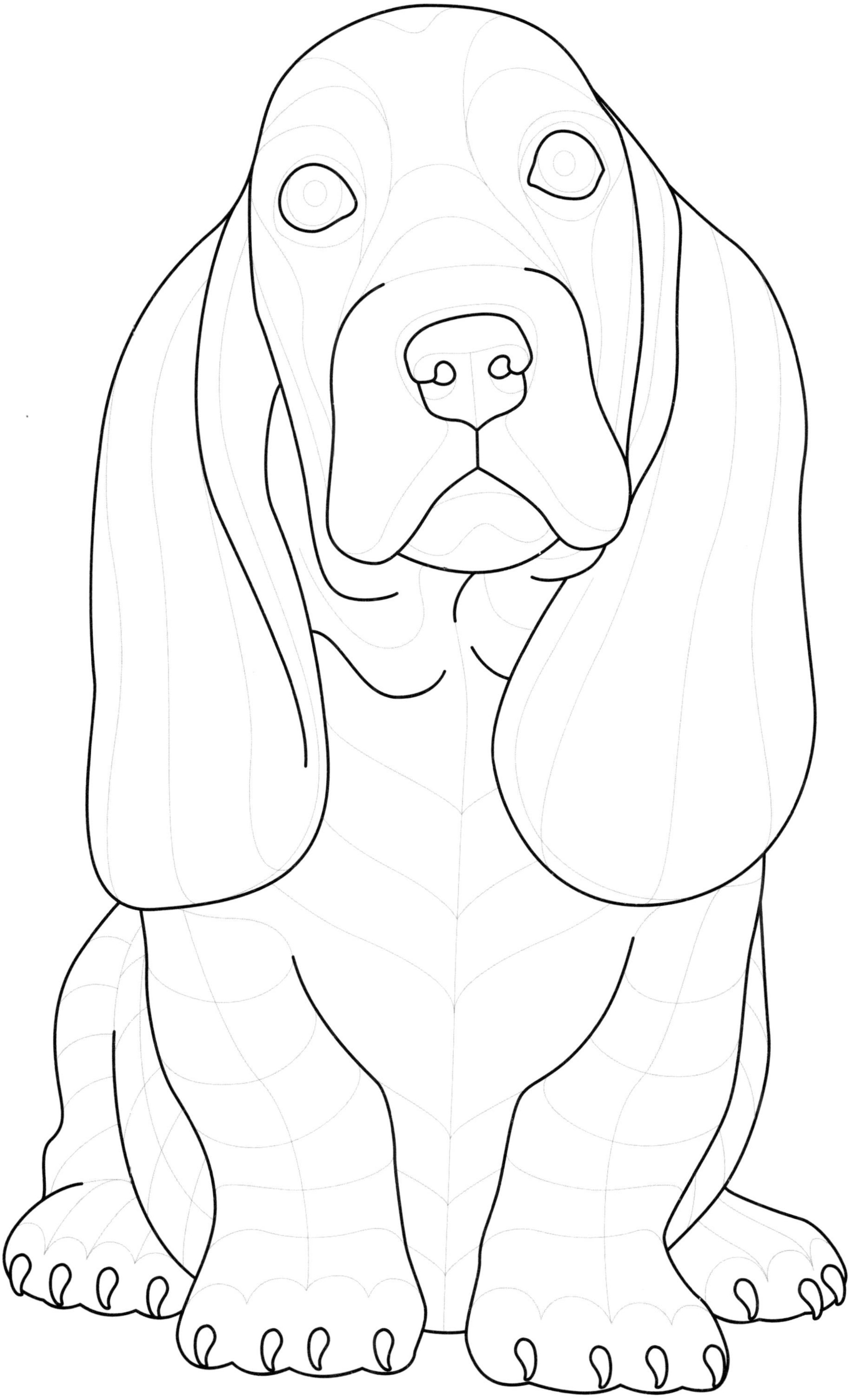

A dog is the only thing on earth that loves you more than he loves himself.

—Josh Billings

DO#1109, Basset Hound:

The basset hound originates in France, where the French word *bas* means "low"—appropriate for a breed that typically only grows to a height of 14 inches (36 cm).

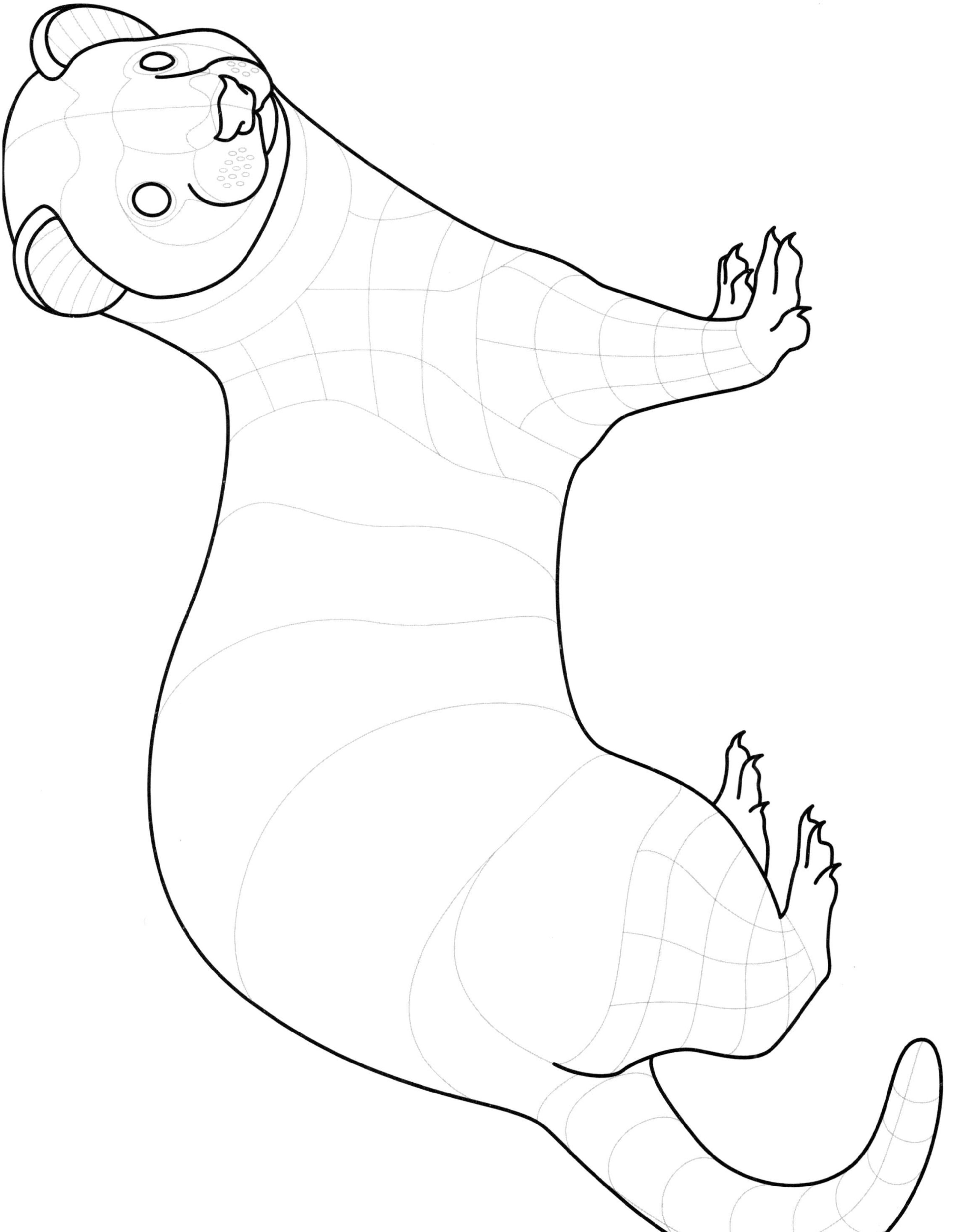

Friendship isn't about whom you have known the longest. It's about who came and never left your side.

—Unknown

DO#1110, Ferret:

The feisty ferret is very playful, but also enjoys dozing for 14 to 18 hours each day.

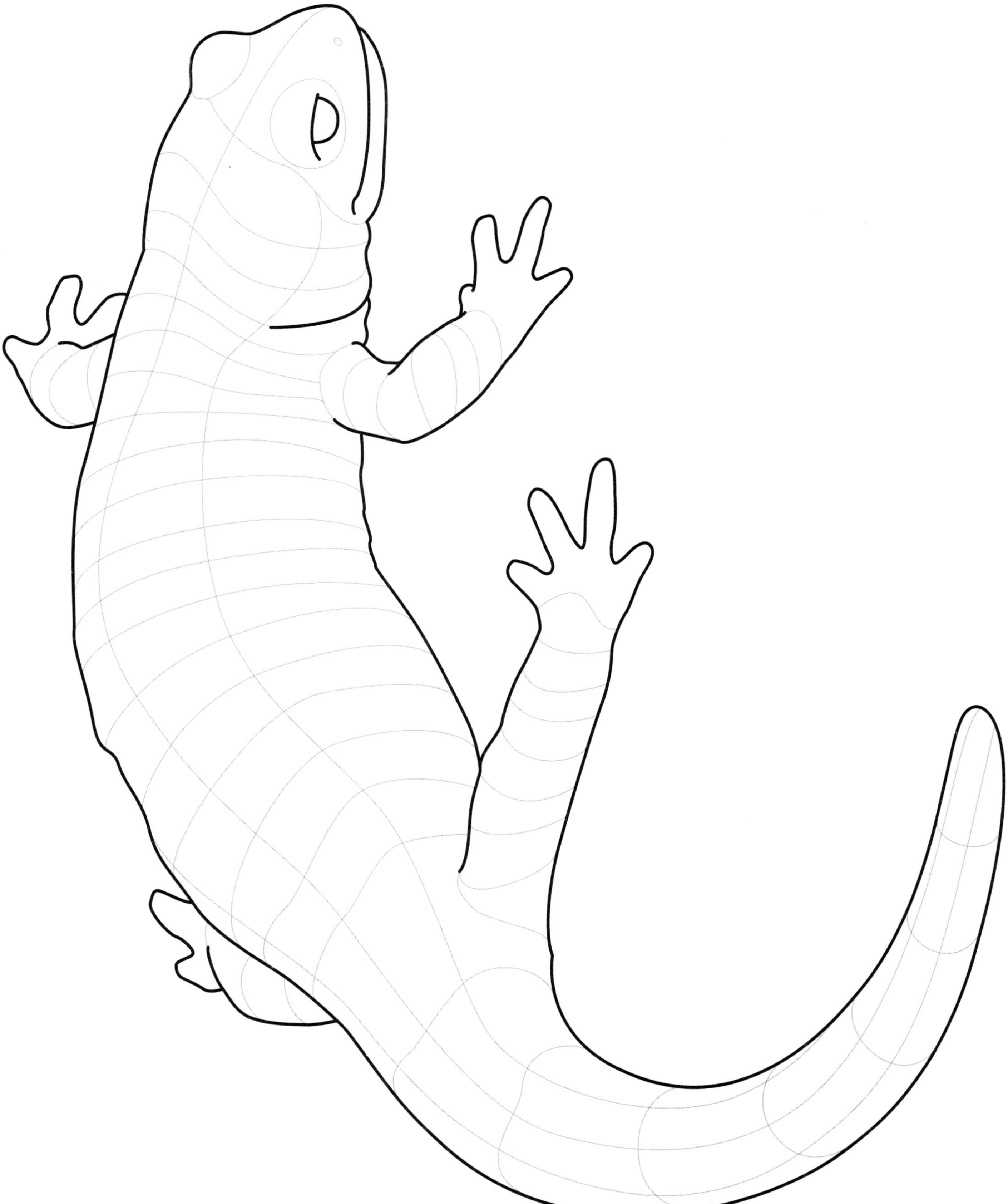

On the outside, we are all different,
but we all have one common thing that should bind us.
A beating heart.

—Unknown

DO#1111, Salamander:

A salamander can regenerate lost limbs in a few weeks, allowing them to survive attacks from predators.

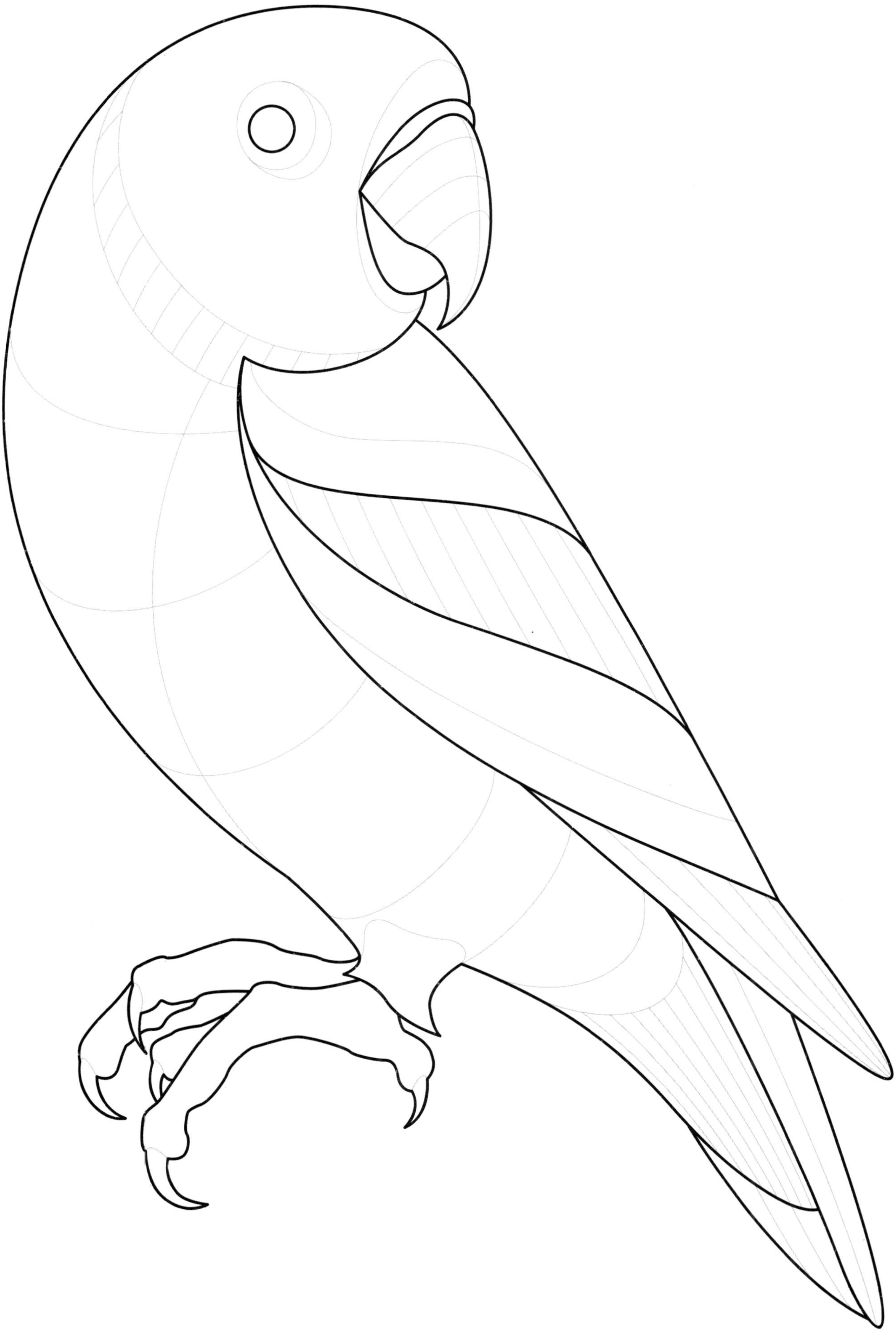

It is amazing how much love and laughter pets bring into our lives and even how much closer we become with each other because of them.

—Josh Grogan

DO#1112, Lovebird:

If a breeding pair of lovebirds has been separated or has experienced a period of stress, they will feed each other to re-establish their bond.

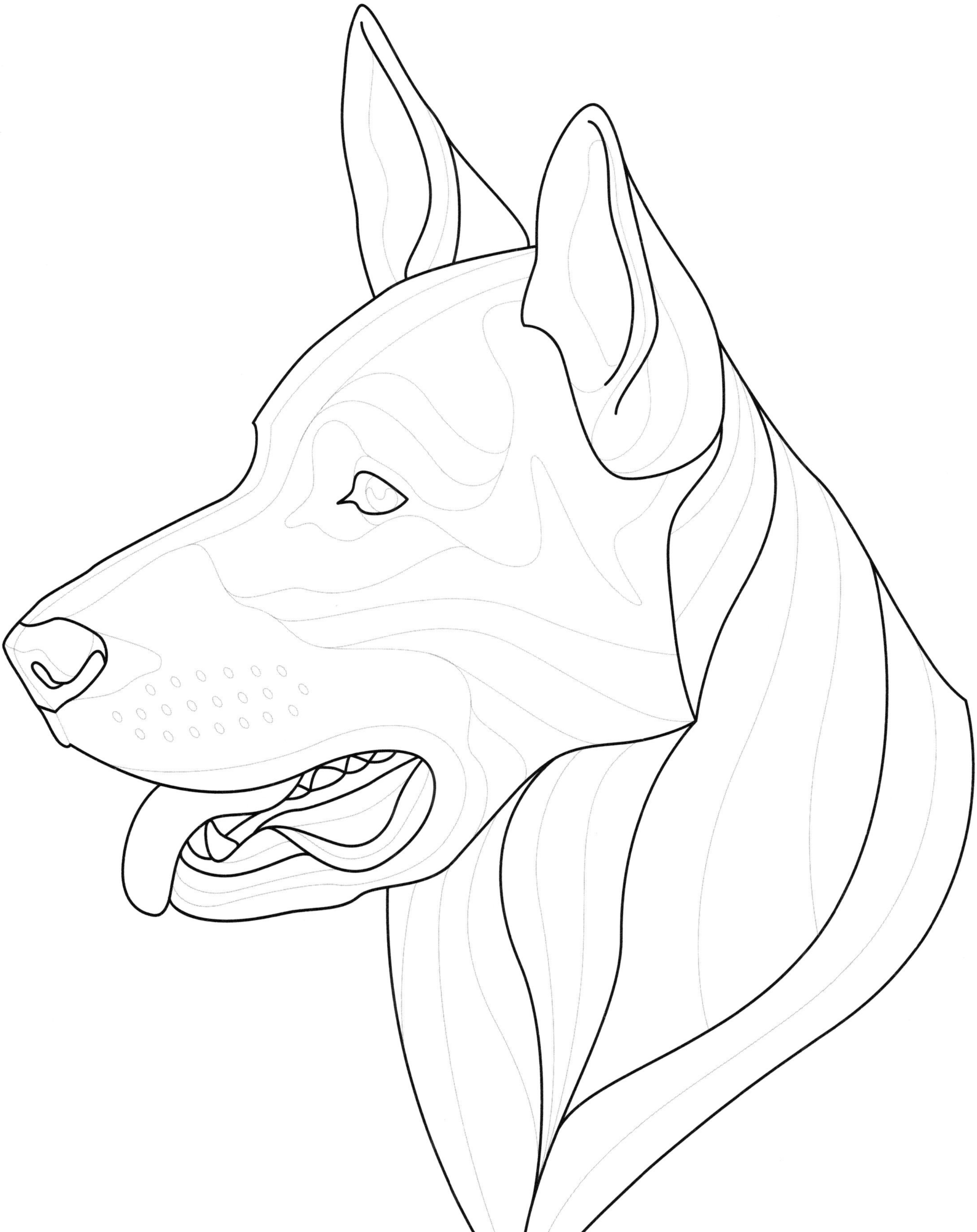

If I could be half the person my dog is,
I'd be twice the human I am.

—Charles Yu

DO#1113, German Shepherd:
German shepherds are popular as family, guard, performance, show, police, military, and service dogs.

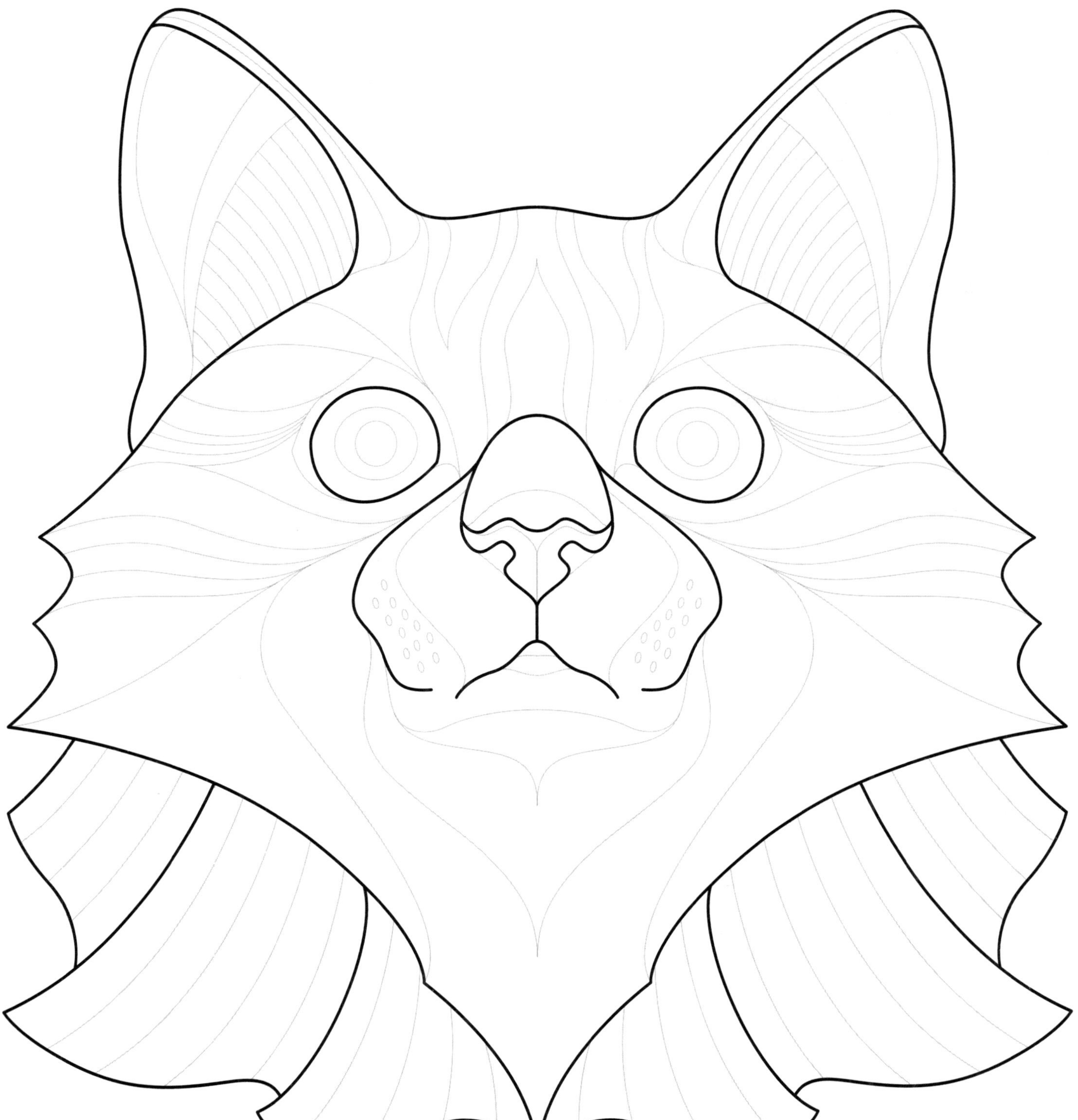

In order to keep a true perspective of one's importance, everyone should have a dog that will worship him and a cat that will ignore him.

—Unknown

DO#1114, Cat:

Cats spend an average of ⅔ of every day sleeping.

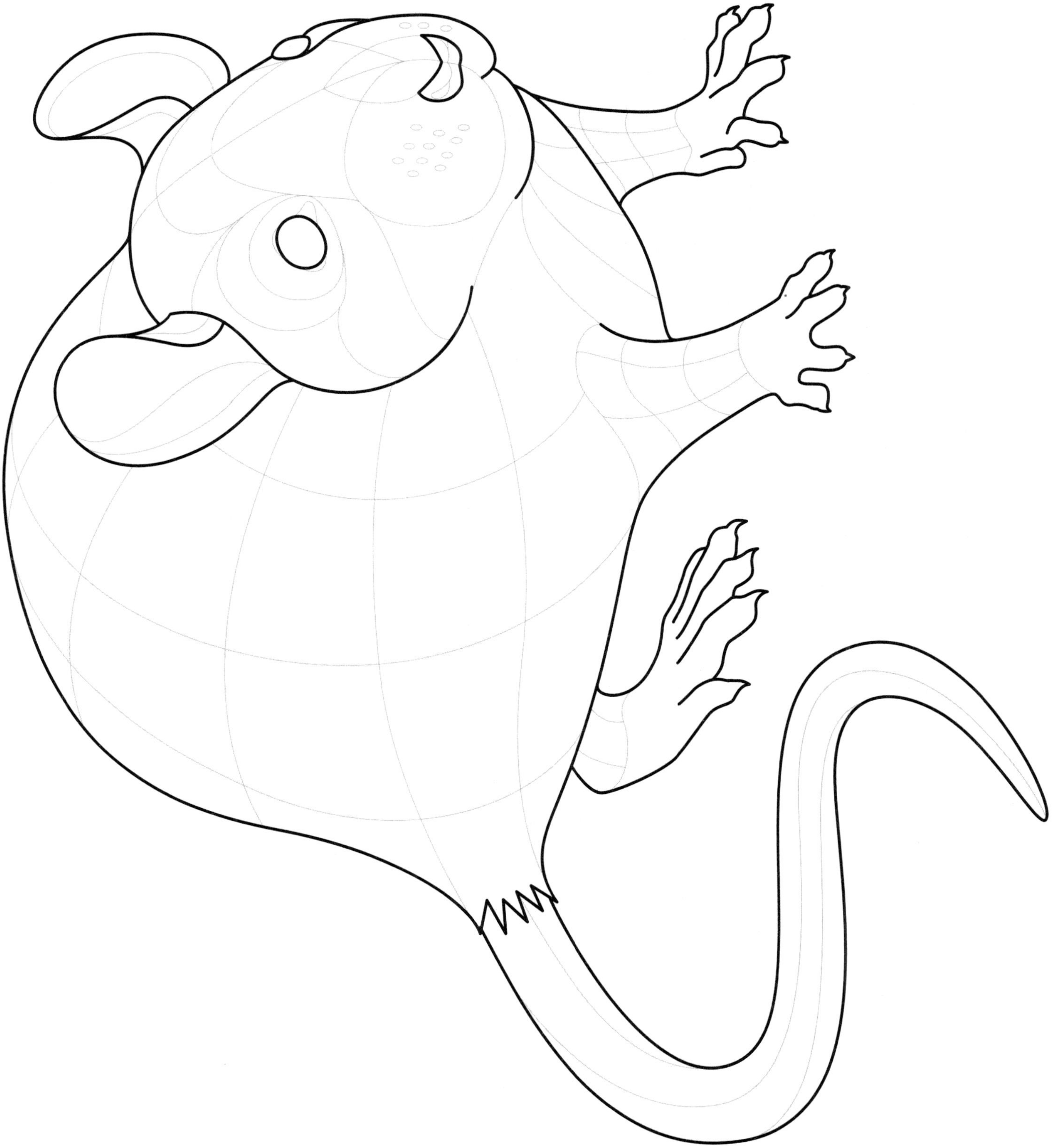

Until one has loved an animal,
a part of one's soul remains unawakened.

—Anatole France

DO#1115, Rat:

The presence of a rat in ancient Rome was thought to be good luck.

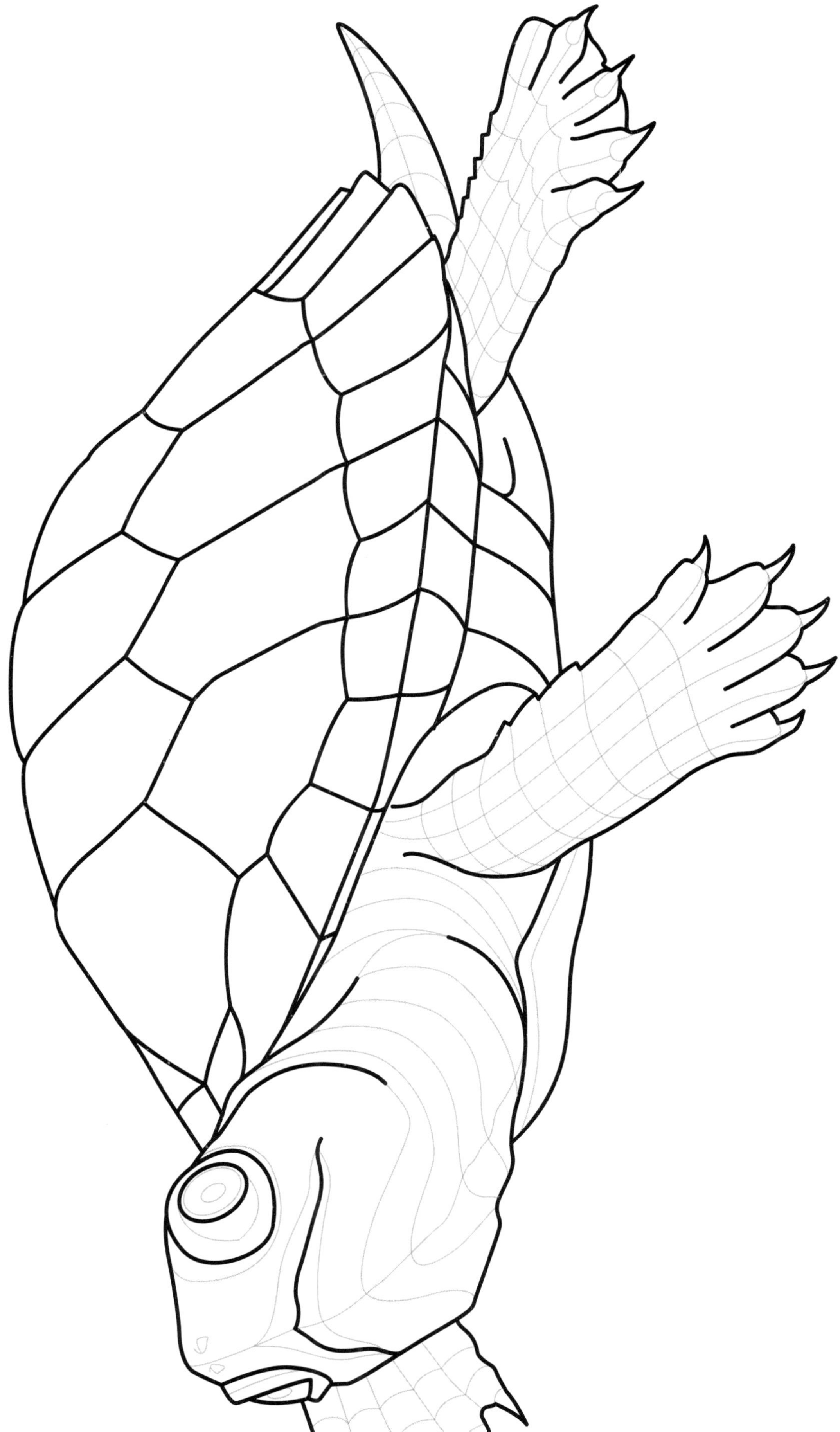

A house is not a home without a pet.

—Unknown

DO#1116, Turtle:

Several species of turtles can live for over 100 years, including the American Box Turtle.

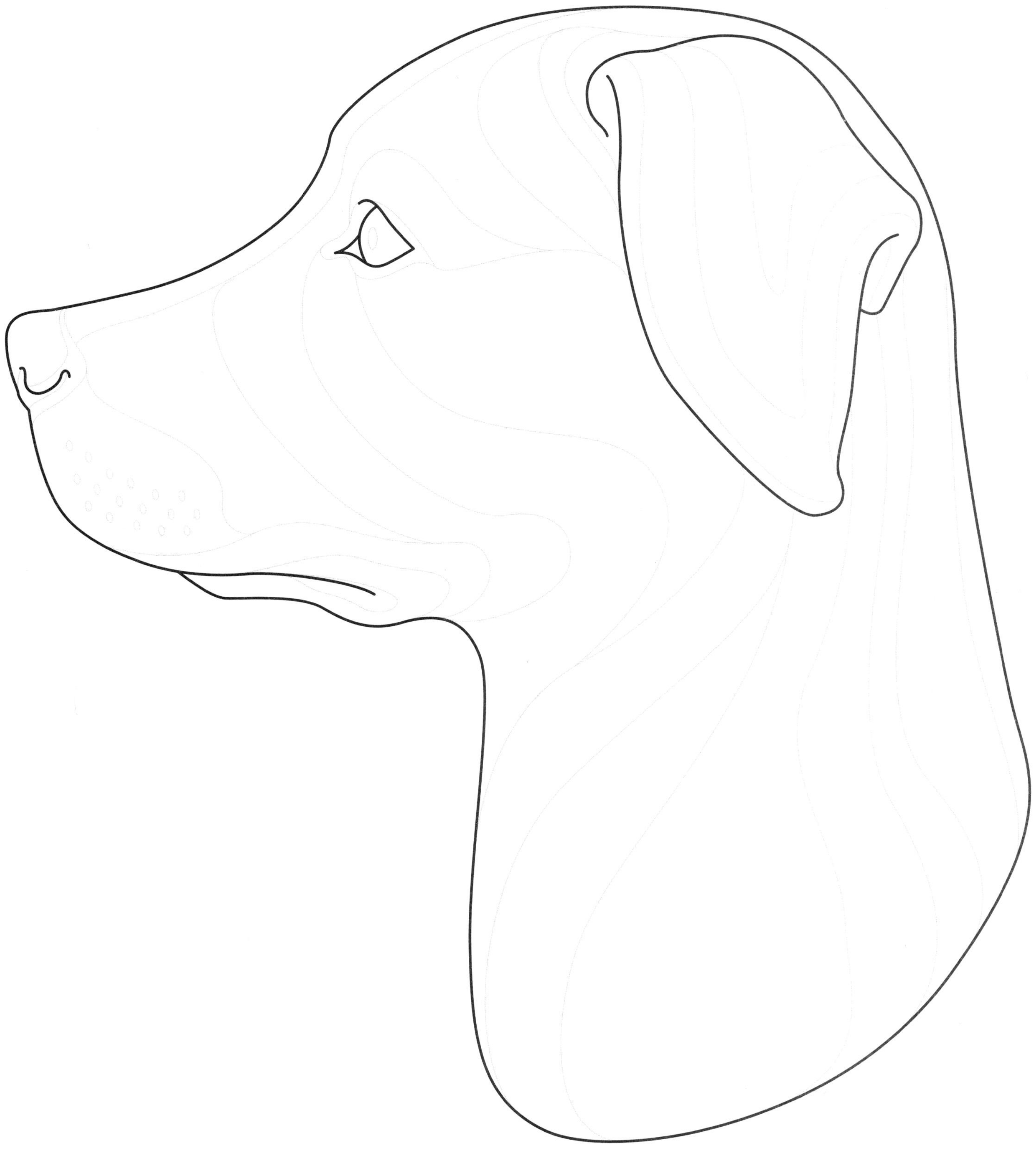

I think dogs are the most amazing creatures;
they give unconditional love. For me,
they are the role model for being alive.

—Gilda Radner

DO#1117, Labrador Retriever:
Labs are known to keep their playful puppy behaviors well into their adult years.

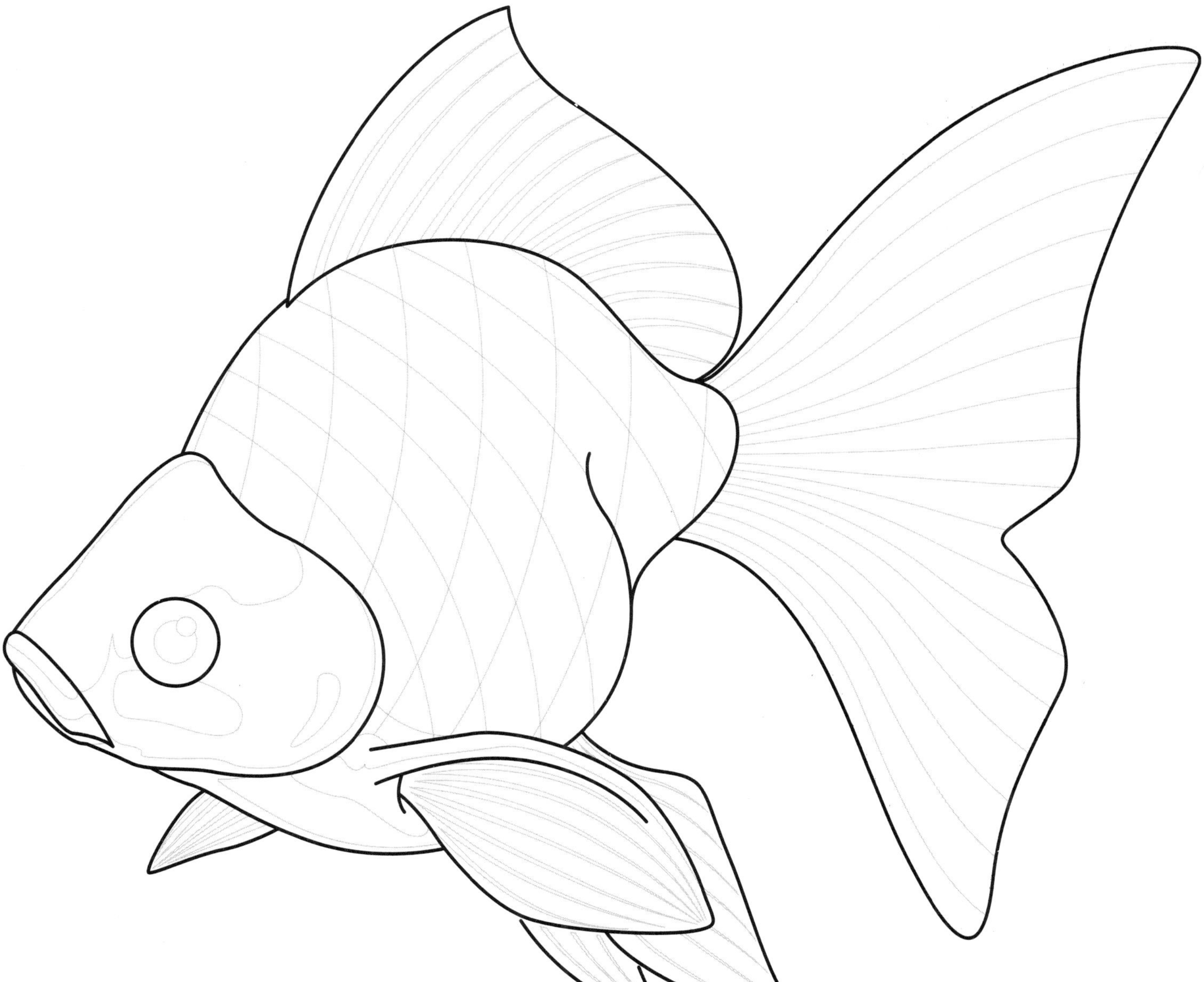

Our task must be to free ourselves by widening our circle of compassion to embrace all living creatures and the whole of nature and its beauty.

—Albert Einstein

DO#1118, Ryukin:

Ryukins are a variety of fancy goldfish that secrete a type of mucus from their skin that provides protection against infections and helps them move through the water faster.

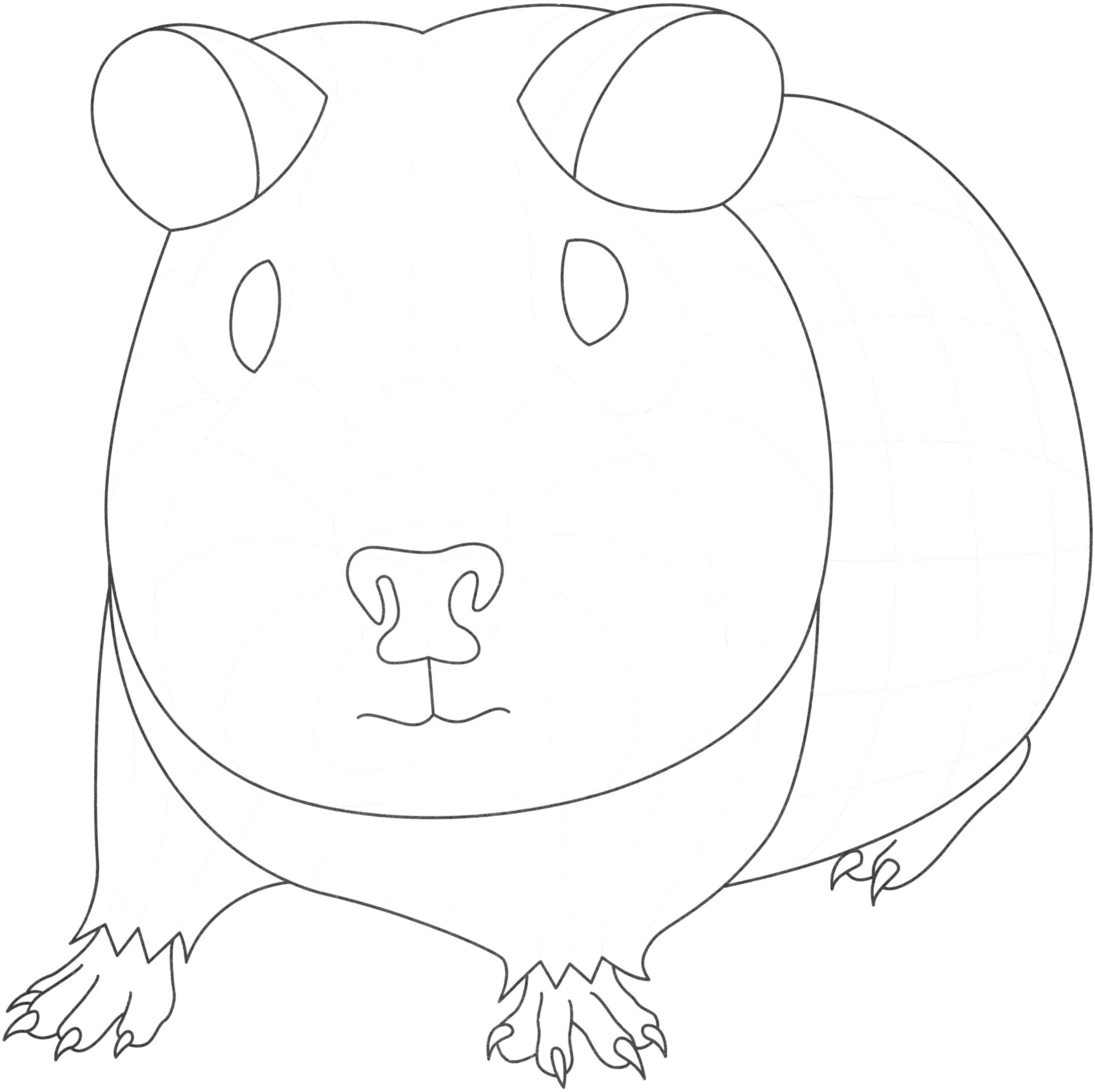

Love is love, whether it goes on two legs or four.

—Gwen Cooper

DO#1119, Guinea Pig:

A male Guinea pig is called a boar,
a female is a sow, and a baby is a pup.

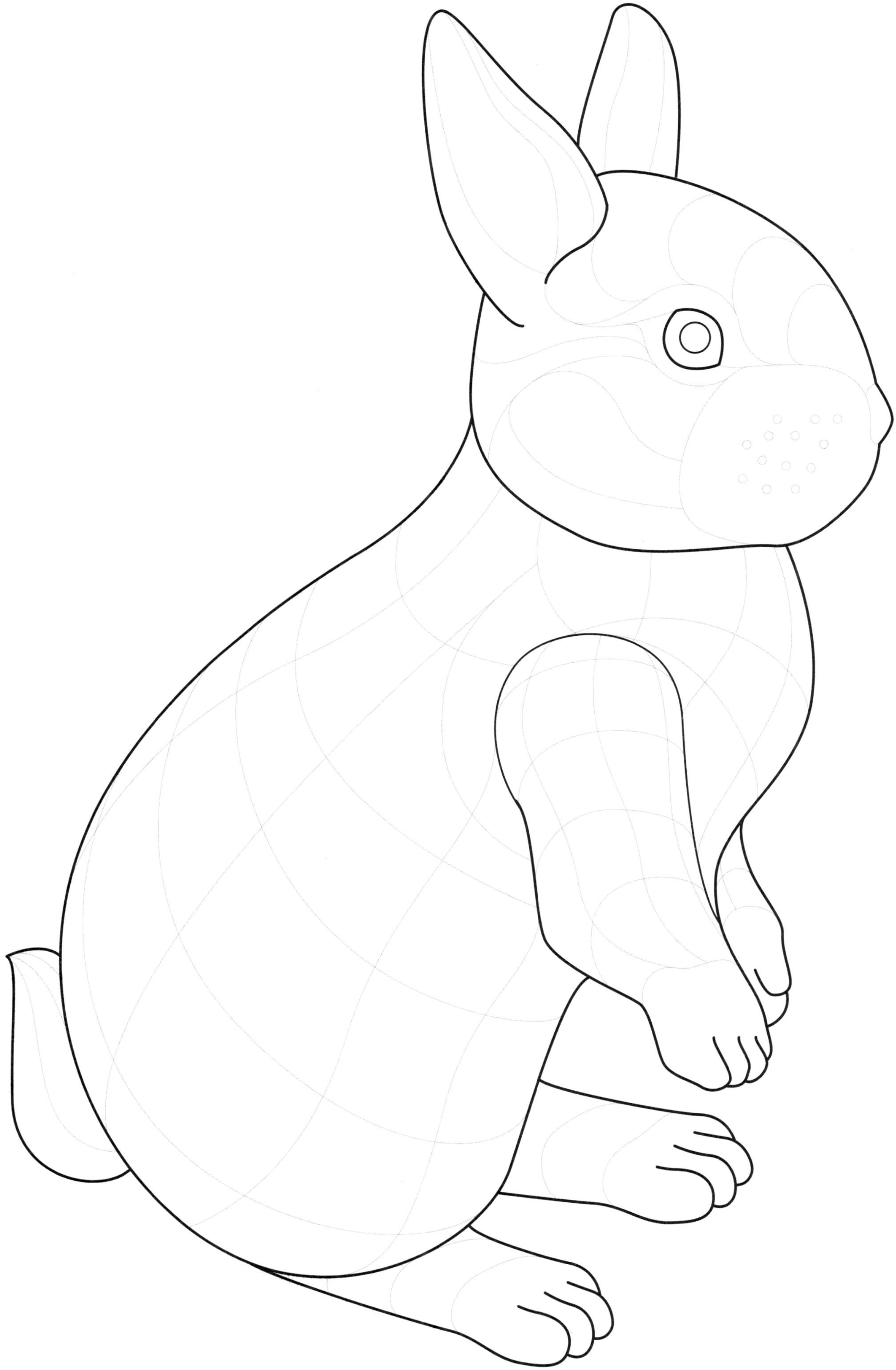

You know, sometimes the world seems like a pretty mean place.
That's why animals are so soft and huggy.

—Bill Watterson, *Calvin & Hobbes*

DO#1120, Bunny:

Rabbits have nearly 360-degree vision, allowing them to see behind them.
Their only blind spot is in front of their nose.

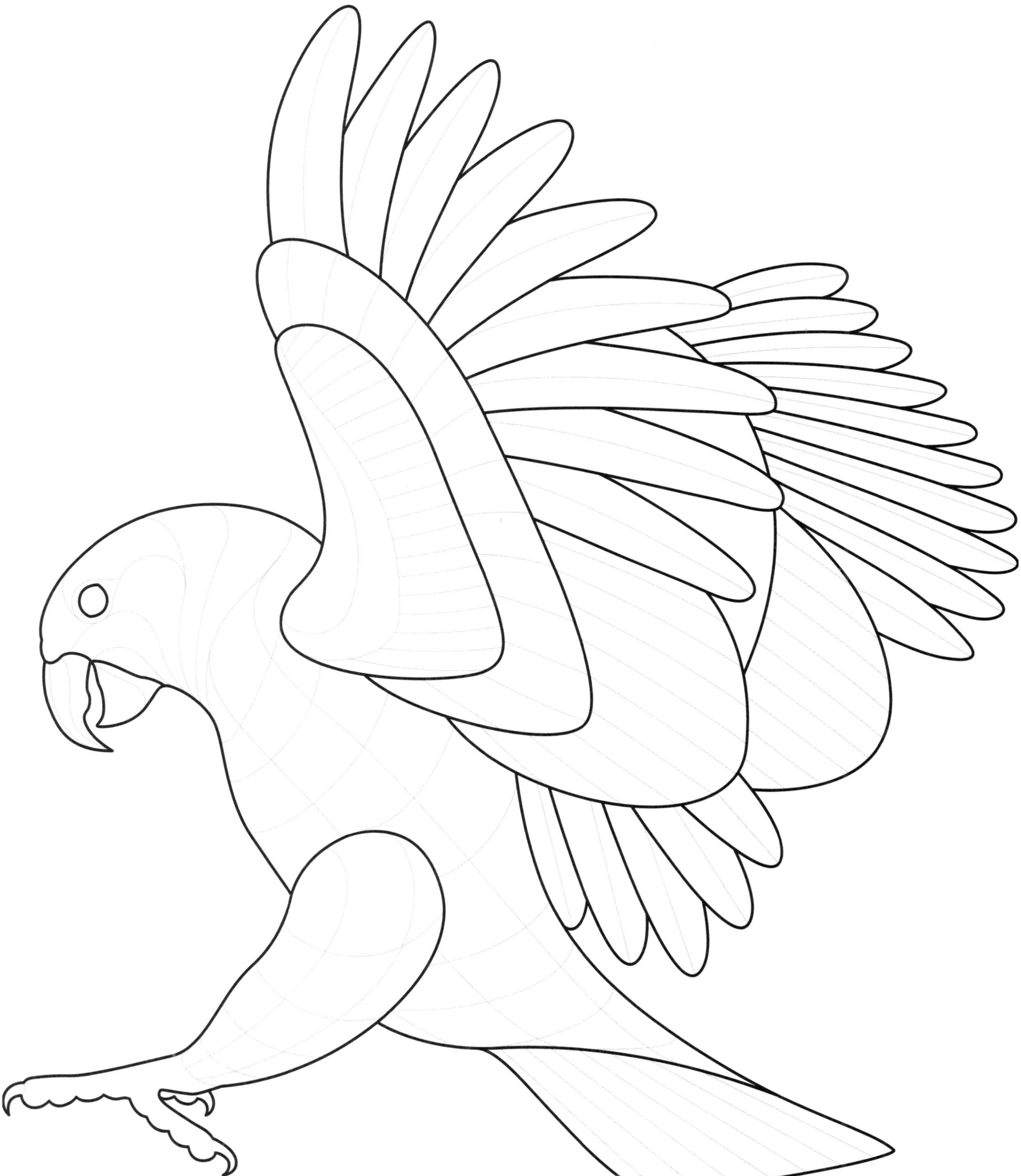

When we love an animal as our family,
we begin to understand animals are our family.

—Anthony Douglas Williams

DO#1121, Parrot:

There are well over 300 species of parrots,
and most live in tropical areas.

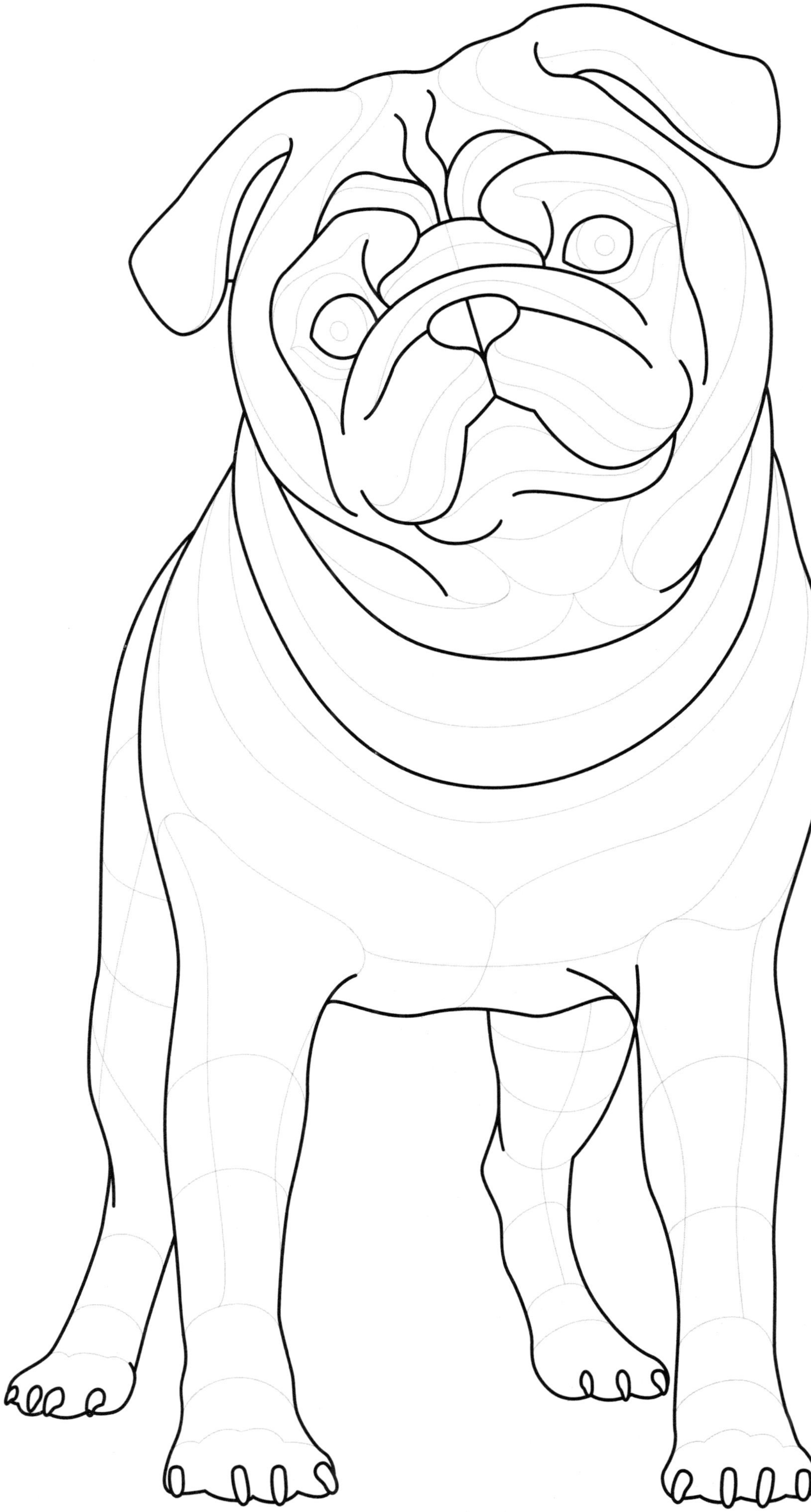

Animals are such agreeable friends—
they ask no questions, they pass no criticisms.

—George Eliot

DO#1122, Pug:

Pugs are ideal apartment dogs, as they are small—
10 to 14 inches (25-36 cm) tall at the shoulder—and require only moderate exercise.

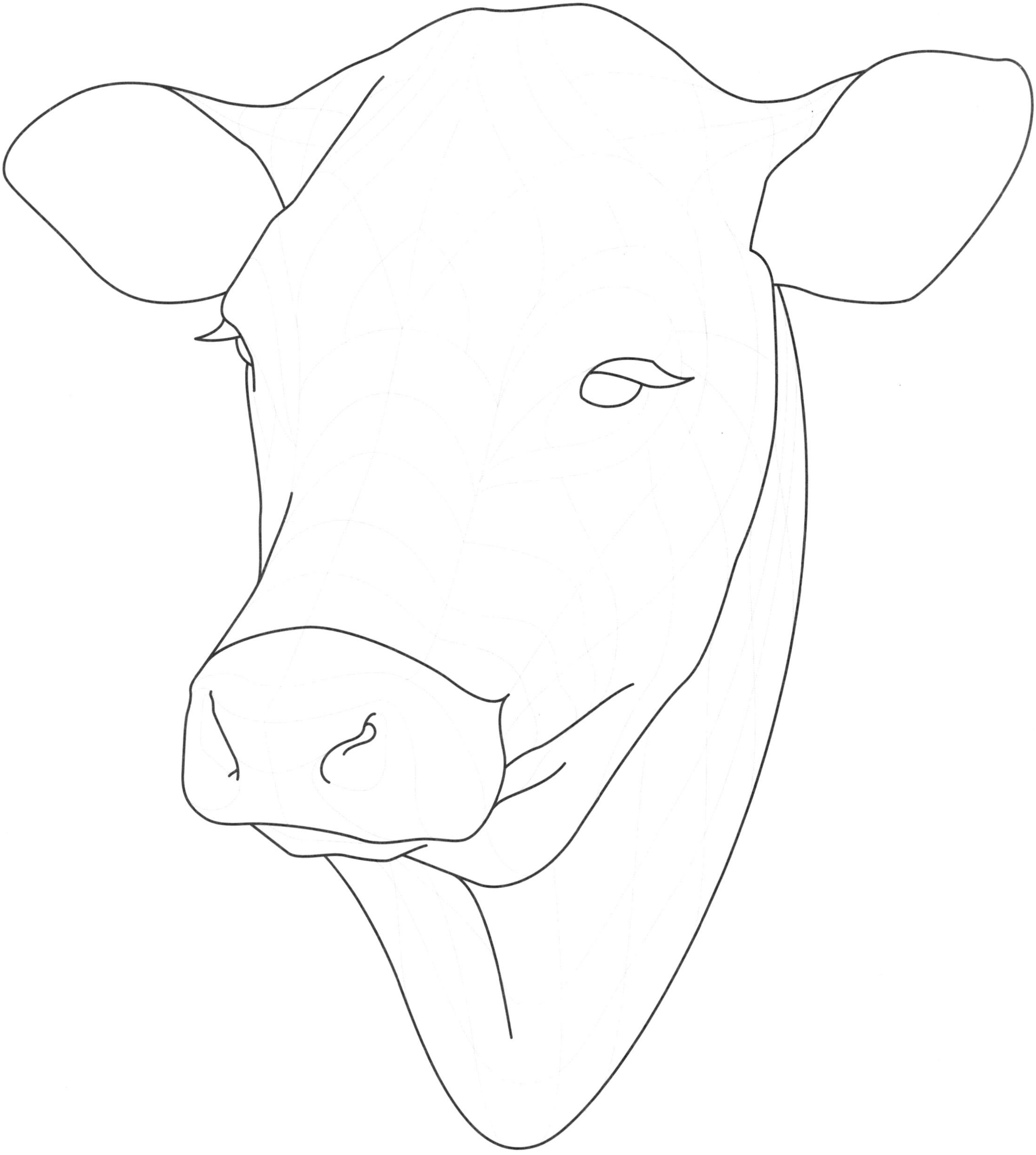

Animals are reliable, many full of love, true in their affections, predictable in their actions, grateful and loyal.

—Alfred A. Montapert

DO#1123, Cow:

In 1611, the first cow arrived in the United States at the Jamestown, Virginia, colony.

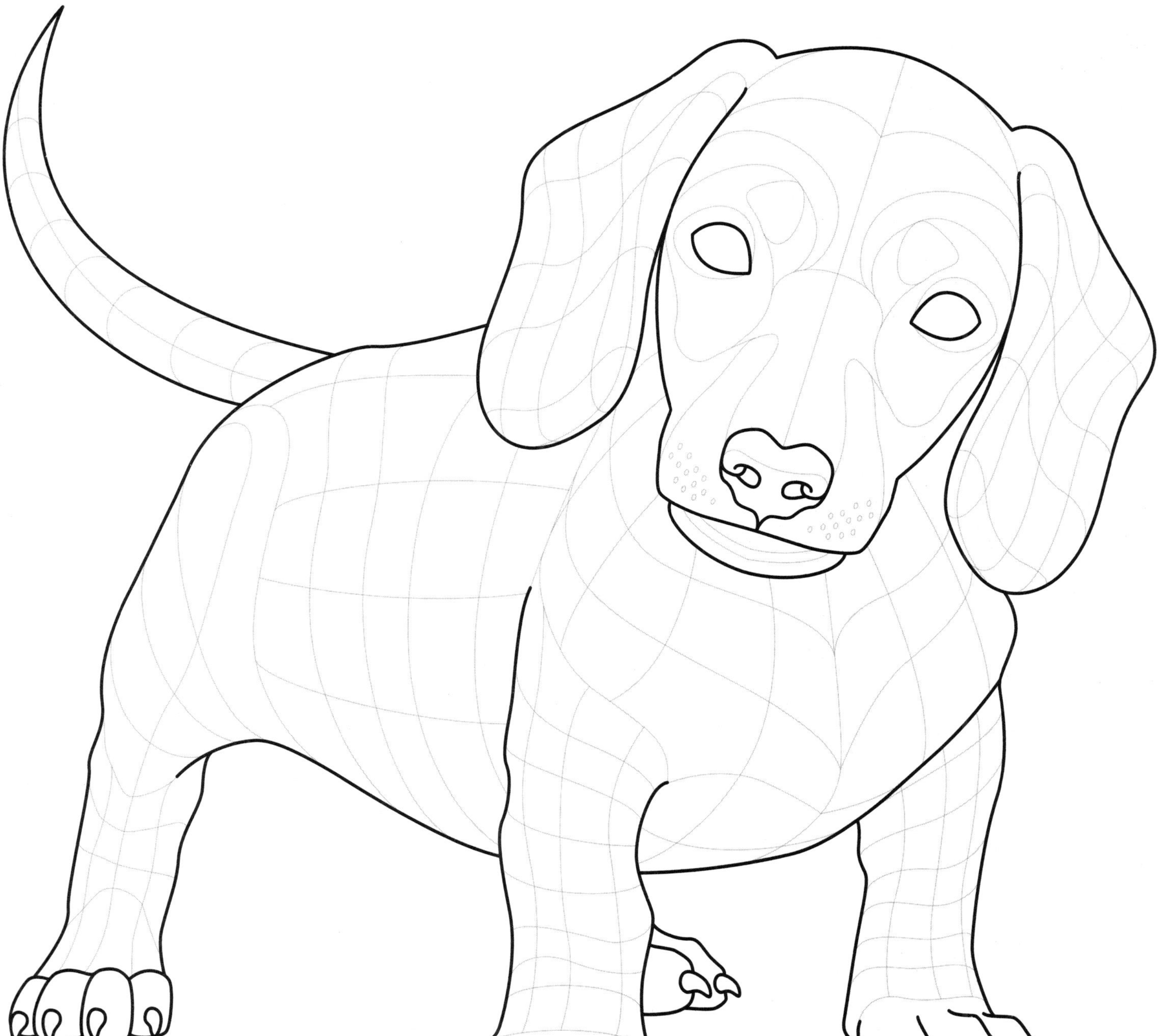

The road to my heart is paved with paw prints.

—Unknown

DO#1124, Dachshund:

These loyal, affectionate, and often stubborn dogs
come in standard and miniature sizes, and have three coat types—
smooth, wirehaired, and longhaired.